I0542624

Outlaw's Secrets

The Outlaw Series: Book 4

By

Sherry Derr-Wille

Published by
Melange Books, LLC
White Bear Lake, MN 55110
www.melange-books.com

ISBN: 978-1-61235-813-0 Print

Cover Art by Lynsee Lauritsen

Outlaw's Secrets
Sherry Derr Wille

For Clay Martin his parents' past is something he knows nothing about. He's hoping a summer spent with his Uncle Gary in Missouri will shed some light on it.

Amy Baines has a secret too, but doesn't know it until Clay comes to town and helps her delve into her forgotten past.

By the time they realize their friendship could lead to more, Clay has gone back to San Francisco and Amy is coming to grips with her St. Louis family. Can they bridge the miles and find love?

I dedicate this book to the fans who support me and the characters who won't let me sleep until their stories are told.

Chapter One

Clay Martin returned to his dorm room. He hated being so far from Virginia City, but his mother insisted if he wanted to become a doctor, the best place to study was in San Francisco.

With the long winter over and his final exams finished, he would soon be able to return home. He missed his mother and father to say nothing of his sister, Ellie.

A banging on the door drew his attention from all thoughts of home. "Are you Dr. Clay Martin?" the messenger boy from the telegraph office questioned.

The only people who called him doctor were his family from Virginia City. He kept telling them he had to finish this year of school and pass all his exams before he could use the word in connection with his name. Hearing this stranger call him doctor told Clay something had to be wrong at home.

"Yes," he replied, apprehension growing.

"This wire is for you." The boy held out a yellow envelope and waited as if in anticipation of a tip for his service.

Clay dug in his pocket for the coins to give the boy so he could have privacy to read whatever was so important to send a wire rather than a letter. As soon as he was alone, he ripped open the yellow envelope. The neatly printed words were like a slap in the face.

PAPA SHOT—NOT EXPECTED TO LIVE—MAMA HAS TAKEN TO HER BED—YOUR RETURN IMPERATIVE
                                        -ELLIE

It seemed as though his heart stopped for several seconds, even though it hadn't. Breathing deeply, he focused on the message from his sister. At times like these, he wished he'd been able to have a telephone installed in his dorm room. Even if he had, he knew his sister wouldn't have been able to make such a call. It was entirely possible Jason was the one to prompt Ellie to send a wire instead.

"Hey Martin, are you just going to stand there by the door?" His roommate Jackson Palmer called as he barged into the room. "They've posted the results of our finals. We're going to go down to the commons and see how we did before we go out and celebrate."

"You go ahead," Clay finally managed to say. "I have to send a wire, talk to the dean, and get a train back home."

"Home? I thought you weren't going until the term ends next week."

"My pa's been shot. If I leave tonight I might be able to get there before he dies."

"Is your ma strong enough to handle something like this?"

Clay didn't have to answer Jackson's inquiry. It was no secret Clay's mother wasn't a strong person.

"That's why I'm going to talk to the dean and go home early. With Pa shot and Ma sick, Ellie will need all the help she can get."

* * * *

The train pulled into Virginia City. Clay picked up his traveling bag and made his way down the aisle toward the door.

As soon as he stepped onto the platform, he breathed deeply, enjoying the crisp mountain air. Before him was the panorama he'd loved all his life. It was a normal homecoming. Normal, except for the fact his parents weren't there to meet him. As he looked around, he saw his sister wasn't among the people waiting for the train. In her stead, Jason Bellinger, his family's longtime friend stepped forward to greet him. Clay wondered if it was his imagination or if Jason had aged since Clay left for school last fall.

"Clay, my boy, it's good to see you," Jason said as he pumped

2

Clay's hand in greeting.

"How are they?" Clay did not really want to hear the answer.

Jason's expression said more than any words. It was as though the man had lost everything that gave his life meaning. "You mother passed away this morning. It was peaceful. I don't think she could have gone on without your father."

Clay felt as though the strength suddenly left his legs. Before he lost control, Jason's bodyguard, Sam, was at Clay's side.

"Come along, son," Sam said. "You pa has been hangin' on 'til you could get here. We're to bring you back to the house."

Clay nodded and allowed the big black man to lead him to the waiting automobile. He'd known Sam and his wife, Sally, all his life. The two of them along with Jason were as close as any family could ever be. Even though Jason ran the elegant gaming club, The Mother Lode, Clay's mother cherished Jason's friendship.

The trip from the train station to the mansion where Clay grew up was made in silence. Clay relished the quiet as his thoughts centered on his father. How could anyone callously shoot down a U.S. Marshal? It was something the family always knew could happen. Clay also knew this was hardly the Wild West he read about in the dime novels his mother never wanted him to read. In 1915, people were more civilized. The modern world was no longer as lawless as the area had once been.

A glance at Jason left no doubt as to the thoughts crowding the man's mind. Whatever the connection with the wealthy gambler and Clay's deeply religious mother, Clay never knew. What he could tell was Jason was devastated by what he considered a personal loss.

The mansion, which usually bustled with activity, was strangely quiet. As though one with the house, Clay's sister, Ellie, appeared before him. Her normally sun darkened skin was a translucent white, making her green eyes and red hair even more striking than usual.

"Mama's gone," she managed to say before allowing him to take her in his arms.

"I know. Jason told me."

"Sally and I were with her. I thought Sally's heart would break the way she cried. She told Mama she was like her own child and she never loved anyone the way she did her."

"What about Pa?"

Ellie began to shake, while tears ran down her cheeks. "It's bad, Clay. He keeps telling me he's going to be all right, but he's not. He's going to die. I know he is. He's only waiting for you to get here. It's best if you go up to see him, so he can stop struggling. This game of pretense is draining him."

Clay kissed the top of his sister's head and then took the stairs two at a time until he reached the second floor of the house. At the top of the stairs, the door to his parents' room stood ajar.

Clay's father, Russ, lay in the big bed. All his life Clay looked up to his father. Russ Martin was always larger than life. Although Clay was as tall as his father he knew he could never measure up to the man he loved and respected.

The man Clay saw lying in the bed was suddenly old, suddenly frail. If it weren't for the slight rise and fall of the sheet, Clay would have thought his father already dead.

"It's me, Pa," Clay said, his voice hardly more than a whisper.

Russ' eyes opened and then focused on Clay. "Jesse's dead. Your ma is gone. I felt her spirit leave."

"I know, Pa."

"I don't have much longer." A fit of coughing cut off his words. It took several moments before he had enough breath to continue. "You and Ellie have to know the truth. The secret must be told."

"What truth, Pa?" Clay was bewildered by his father's words.

"Your mother's Bible. Promise me you and Ellie will read the papers it holds once I'm gone. If you have any questions, Gary will answer them."

"Gary?" Clay frowned.

Russ nodded and then closed his eyes. Clay listened as his father drew his last breath. Unwilling to release Russ' hand, Clay sat by the bed for nearly an hour.

"What were you talking about, Pa? Who is Gary? What's hidden in Ma's Bible?"

"Just the truth about who your mother was." Clay turned to see Jason standing in the doorway. "Is your father gone?"

Clay nodded. "He died just after I got here. I—I ..." Unmanly tears

4

kept the rest of the words from passing his lips.

He was barely aware of Jason helping him to his feet and guiding him down the stairs to the parlor where Ellie waited for him.

* * * *

Two caskets were lowered into the double grave, which had been dug in the cemetery overlooking the mansion.

"Dear Lord," the minister said, as clumps of dirt clattered against the tops of the wooden caskets. "We commit the bodies of our brother, Russell, and our sister, Jesse, to the ground and their souls to your loving care."

Ellie's soft sobs tore at Clay's heart. As he held her close, he couldn't help but remember Jason's promise to tell him about the truth his father mentioned with his dying breath.

With all the preparations for the funeral, Clay hadn't found the time to search his mother's Bible for the answers to the questions his father's settlement provoked.

Clay turned from the grave. For the first time, he took note of the people who came to say their final farewells to his parents. The elite of Virginia City as well as the surrounding area stood shoulder to shoulder with U.S. Marshals, miners and saloon girls.

One by one, the people left the hill where the sun baked the soil rock hard. Within minutes only Jason, Sam, and Sally remained with Clay and Ellie.

"It's time to get you two lambs back to the house," Sally said. "Mr. Jason says the time is right for you to know who your mama and papa were before they came to Virginia City."

Ellie looked as though she had no idea what Sally was talking about. Could it be their father only told Clay of the secrets hidden in his mother's worn Bible only two days earlier?

Obediently, Clay and Ellie followed the three older people down the hill to the waiting carriage. It only seemed fitting for Sam to have brought the team and carriage rather than the car to the cemetery. For one thing, the road was too rocky for the automobile to maneuver. Sam drove while Jason and Clay sat beside him on the wide seat. Behind them, Sally comforted Ellie while she cried.

After Sally served a lunch of cold sliced beef and fresh bread along with some aged cheese and soup, they all took their coffee into the parlor.

"I've purposely waited until now to tell you the truth about your parents," Jason began. "Your mother deserved to have you mourn her without the judgment of what I have to say may bring."

"Judgment?" Ellie echoed. "What are you talking about?"

"Before your mother became Jesse Martin, she led many different lives. As Laurel Morgan she was the toast of Virginia City."

"Laurel Morgan?" Clay interrupted. "I've heard of her. She was one of the girls ..." He left the rest of his realization unspoken.

It was no wonder his mother never told them about her past. She must have been ashamed of being one of Jason's whores.

Before he could storm from the room, Sam stopped him. "Miss Laurel wasn't no whore," he declared as though he read Clay's thoughts.

"She was a poor frightened child," Sally interjected. "I thank the Lord every day that it was Mr. Jason who found her on that riverboat and not someone else. By the looks of the two of you, she never told you about it. I know you want to run off and hide like two scared kittens, but you will hear Mr. Jason out."

Clay took a deep breath and then clasped Ellie's hand. "I guess we don't have much choice."

Jason smiled. Before starting again, he poured himself another cup of coffee.

"I met Laurel on a riverboat trip from New Orleans to Dubuque. She was a beautiful woman, who in actuality was little more than a frightened child. It didn't take long for me to see through the story she told about her limp coming from a riding accident."

Clay thought about the story, which was so much a part of his mother. She'd explained her need for a cane by telling them of a tragic accident she'd had as a young girl. Now Jason was telling them it was all a lie.

He listened as Jason continued to tell him about Jessie Tyler, the outlaw's daughter, and how one of her father's men shot her in the back. Names like Caleb, Frank, Will, Ed, Clay, and Gary Tyler permeated the narrative.

The stories of bank robberies sickened Clay. He couldn't stop either his tears or his anger, when he learned he carried the name of his dead uncle, an uncle who was hanged for murder before his twentieth birthday. Even more devastating was to learn his sister was named for his father's first wife, who had been killed by the Tyler gang.

"It was your mother's faith that brought her through those terrible years of riding with your grandfather," Jason ended.

"Are you certain about this?" Clay finally managed to say.

Jason nodded. "After your parents returned from their wedding trip, a writer from San Francisco contacted them. Your father convinced Jesse to talk to the man. When he was done, the Tyler gang was immortalized in a dime novel."

For the first time, Clay understood why his mother disagreed with his love for the tales of the old west. He couldn't help but wonder what would have happened if he'd read the story of his family in a book.

"Your mother agreed to the writing of the story only if the book wouldn't be distributed in San Francisco or in Virginia City. She did keep a copy of it for herself. I don't know if she thought it was the last link to her family or a bitter reminder of her past. Whichever it was, I know she read it only once, but kept it hidden away from the two of you."

Jason reached into the inner pocket of his jacket and produced a book that looked like it was never opened, to say nothing of being read. Clay took the book and looked at the cover. His mother's face stared back at him. Behind her stood six men, half of them looked like his mother while the other half bore a strong resemblance to the older man who stood in their midst.

"None of them can hurt either of you," Jason said. He pointed to the youngest of the six. "This is your Uncle Gary. He's the only one left alive."

The name Gary brought back the memory of his father saying Gary would explain everything.

"Your mother kept in touch with her brother, but refused to let him contact you."

"Why wouldn't she want us to know her family?" Ellie pleaded, speaking for the first time since Jason began his explanation.

"As much as Jesse and Gary loved each other, her past was so painful she decided to hide it from you. Although they corresponded, she never mentioned either of you. We all tried to convince her to change her mind. Several times I pushed your father to tell Gary, but he respected and loved your mother too much to go against her wishes."

Jason continued to explain Jesse's reasons for keeping the truth of her past from Clay and Ellie, but Clay hardly listened. Throughout the afternoon, he fingered the cover of the book written about his family.

When Jason, Sam, and Sally finally left the mansion, Ellie went directly to bed. As tired as Clay was earlier, he found he couldn't sleep. Instead, he prepared for bed, then propped up with pillows began to read the book his mother never wanted him to see. It was well past midnight when he read the last words and put the book aside.

The account read more like a news story than a sensationalized story romanticizing the lives of outlaws and hired gunmen. The thought of his delicate mother living such a life made him sick. He wondered how much of what he just read was true. With both his mother and father dead, only his Uncle Gary remained.

Since he didn't have to return to school until the fall when his work in the hospital began, Clay knew how he would spend his summer. A trip to Loveland, Missouri would be more than a vacation. It was high time he found his family and confirmed the story he'd just read and found hard to believe.

Chapter Two

Loveland, Missouri

"I need you to deliver a wire for me," Amy's mother said.

Amy Baines closed the account book she'd been working on all morning. The high point of her day was when she was asked to take a telegram to someone from outside of town.

Fifteen years ago, when Amy was six, her father died, though she never knew exactly what happened. What she did know was she and her mother moved away from house they shared with her father. Amy's mother told her of the grandfather who didn't want anything to do with either his daughter-in-law or his granddaughter. In the midst of the story were the vile names her grandfather used to describe the mother Amy loved more than anyone else in the world.

"Amy Marie, did you hear me?"

Hearing her mother call her by both her names brought Amy out of her memories and back to the present. "Yes, Mother, I did hear you. I'm just putting the book away."

"Good, because this wire is important. When you get Mollie saddled, take it out to Mr. Tyler and wait for an answer."

Amy took the yellow envelope from her mother and hurried out to the stable located behind the telegraph office. Fourteen years ago, Amy and her mother left St Louis. Although her mother worked as a maid in one of the many St. Louis mansions, she was somehow able to secure a job working in a telegraph office in Loveland, Missouri.

Amy forced the troubling thoughts of the past from her mind as she led Molly from her stall. After swinging into the saddle, Amy turned toward the Tyler farm.

Mr. Tyler was known for raising fine horses. Amy enjoyed going out there with wires. She appreciated the beautiful horses grazing in Mr. Tyler's pasture.

"Hey Amy," Eli called from the corral by the house. "Is this a social visit? If so, Becky will be pleased to see you."

"I wish it was," Amy replied. "I do have to get out to see her, just not today. Is your father home?"

"I think he'd down at the barn. Why don't you stop and see Becky while I get him?"

Amy dismounted and made her way to the house. Becky McPherson had been one of her best friends in school. When she married Eli last fall, Amy had been happy for her friend while at the same time she was envious.

"Amy," Becky called as soon as she stepped out onto the porch. "It's wonderful to see you. Can we offer you some coffee?"

Amy glanced toward the barn, but Mr. Tyler was nowhere in sight. "I guess I have time."

Becky's mother-in-law, Clara, poured Amy a cup of coffee and cut a generous piece of pie. "I don't suppose you know what's in the wire," she said.

"No, Mrs. Tyler, I don't. You know Mama wouldn't ever tell me what a wire contains. Even if I'd taken the wire, I couldn't tell anyone other than the person whom it was meant for what it contains. She did say it was important, and I should wait for a reply."

"Maybe it's from Laura," Becky suggested. "Maybe she had the baby early."

"Maybe it's best if we read the wire Amy brought us."

Amy liked the way Mr. Tyler took charge. Without hesitation, she handed him the yellow envelope. She watched as he read the contents of the wire. Instead of the joy over the news of a new grandchild, she saw the color drain from his face and sadness cover him like a dark cloud.

"What is it Gary?" Clara prompted.

As though the printed words left him speechless, Mr. Tyler handed the wire to his wife.

JESSIE AND RUSS DEAD—JESSE'S KIDS CLAY AND ELLIE KNOW THE TRUTH—CLAY WANTS TO COME TO LOVELAND—PLEASE ADVISE

–JASON

By the time Clara read the last words, she was sobbing. Whoever these people were, their passing certainly had a devastating effect on the Tyler family.

"Who are Clay and Ellie?" Eli said.

"They're your cousins. Your Aunt Jesse must have wanted to shield them from the ugliness of our past. I can't believe she's gone as well as Russ. I can't be the last of them, I just can't. Jesse was younger than me. It's not fair. It's just not fair."

Amy knew the conversation between father and son was one she had no right to hear. "Is there an answer?" she finally said.

"Oh yes, yes of course," Gary replied once he regained his composure.

Amy reached into her pocket and produced the stub of a pencil along with a pad of paper.

CLAY WELCOME—SORRY TO HEAR OF JESSE AND RUSS' PASSING—YOUR LOSS IS AS GREAT AS MINE—LET US KNOW WHEN TO EXPECT CLAY

-GARY

Amy quickly counted the words and calculated the charges. As soon as Gary gave her the money to pay for the wire, Amy left the Tyler kitchen.

Once she mounted Molly, she turned toward town. She pondered the meaning of the conversation she'd heard. She wondered what could be so ugly about the past this person named Jesse would hide it from her children or her children from people as nice as the Tylers.

* * * *

"What do you know about the Tylers, Mama?" Amy prompted as she helped her mother prepare supper.

Della looked up from the potatoes she was peeling. "About as much

11

as I do about anyone else in town. They mind their business, and I do the same. Why do you ask?"

"The wire I took out there was about Mr. Tyler's sister."

"Amy Marie Baines! How could you? A telegram is private. How many times do I have to tell you not to pry into other people's business? I thought you were serious about taking over here when I'd too old to do the work anymore."

Della's accusations hurt more than Amy cared to admit. "I didn't pry. Mrs. Tyler read the wire aloud. When she did, Mr. Tyler said something about the past being ugly. How can anyone as nice as Mr. Tyler have an ugly past?"

"It's none of our business, Amy," Della admonished. "It's not our place to snoop into other folks' lives. Whatever Mr. Tyler was talking about, it's of no concern to us. Now, get this table set so we can eat."

"Yes, Mama," Amy replied.

As she set the table, she contemplated the events of the morning. Maybe when this Clay, whoever he was, arrived in town she'd learn more. In the meantime, there was nothing standing in the way of her snooping through the back issues of the local newspaper.

From the room beyond the kitchen, the telegraph keys began to click. Leaving her mother to keep an eye on the simmering kettles, Amy went in to write down the message.

WILL TELL CLAY OF YOUR RESPONSE—THIS IS ALL NEW TO HIM—THANK YOU FOR UNDERSTANDING

-JASON

"Looks like I'll be making another trip to the Tyler farm after supper," Amy said, as she saw down across from her mother.

"I don't like you going out after dark. I don't suppose it could wait until morning."

Amy smiled broadly. "I don't suppose it could." Even if it could wait, this was an excellent opportunity to learn more about the ugly past Mr. Tyler mentioned.

* * * *

The sun was just setting when Amy arrived at the Tyler farm. There were lights in the barn, but Mr. Tyler sat on the porch.

"I didn't expect to see you tonight, Amy," he greeted her. "Am I right in thinking you've brought out another wire?"

"Yes sir, I have. It could have waited until morning, but I thought your family might want to answer it tonight."

Mr. Tyler got up from the rocker and made his way to where Amy was dismounting. "And your interest was piqued when you were here earlier. I don't blame you none. If I'd heard what you did, I'd want to ask questions."

Amy sensed a blush creep into her cheeks. "Mama says I'm too snoopy for my own good."

Mr. Tyler laughed and then took the yellow envelope Amy handed him. "From the looks of this wire, the past will be rehashed in this town all summer. Sooner or later, you'll hear the story. While I'm writing a reply, maybe we should talk."

By the time Amy was back on the road to town, she'd heard the most incredible story. Soft-spoken Mr. Tyler had been a member of a notorious outlaw gang with a price on his head. Even his younger sister, Clay Martin's mother, had ridden with the gang. As hard as the story was to believe, it had a ring of truth. Amy knew a trip to the newspaper office would either confirm or deny the tale she'd just heard.

* * * *

"It's all true, Mama," Amy declared over lunch the next day. "Everything Mr. Tyler told me last night is substantiated in the Gazette. Mr. Tyler's father and brother were hanged right here in Loveland."

"I told you last night, it's none of our concern. We're no more part of this town than we were of St. Louis. It's best if we keep to ourselves and not meddle in the lives of others."

Della's words hurt. More than anything else, Amy wanted to be part of the community. The fact Mr. Tyler confided in her said she had his trust. What was it her mother feared? No one here treated them the way her mother said Grandpa Baines did. Her mother's ability on the telegraph key was respected by the people of Loveland. Respect and friendship should go hand in hand. So why was her mother so stubborn that she wouldn't allow herself or Amy to become acquainted with their neighbors?

Amy had little time to dwell on the question, as the telegraph key began to click out a message. Getting up from the table, she quickly transformed the coded message to printed words.

> *ARRIVING NOON TRAIN A WEEK FROM NEXT TUESDAY—*
> *ELLIE TOO DISTRAUT TO TRAVEL—JASON FEELS IT'S*
> *BEST SHE REMAIN IN VIRGINIA CITY—I AM PLANNING TO*
> *SPEND THE SUMMER*
>
> *–CLAY MARTIN*

Amy reread the neatly printed words before folding the paper and putting it in the yellow envelope. "I'll take this wire out to Mr. Tyler."

"If it wasn't business, I'd be concerned about all the trips you've been making out there. It's evident you've always been taken with Eli Tyler. I can see nothing healthy in you being out there getting all crazy over a married man."

"Mama!" Ellie exclaimed. "I can't believe you would say such a thing. Eli is Becky's husband and she's my best friend. I don't know why you're so against me making friends. I'm not looking for a husband and, even if I was, it wouldn't be someone who married to my best friend."

Without waiting for her mother's reply, Amy stormed out of the house. She half-expected Della to follow her, but thankfully her mother stayed inside while Amy saddled Molly.

Chapter Three

"Next stop, Loveland, Missouri," the train conductor announced as he made his way down the aisle past the seat Clay occupied.

Clay's stomach lurched along with the train. It had been a lonely trip. He'd read the journals and news reports so many times, he'd committed them to memory. In a few minutes, he would confront the uncle he didn't know about three weeks ago. There were so many questions Clay wanted answers to and was afraid to learn.

From his mother's diaries, he calculated his uncle's age to be forty-seven. Not old by modern standards, yet neither was his mother, and she was dead.

Clay waited until the other passengers got off before he gathered up his traveling bag and prepared to leave. A cool breeze came as a welcome relief after the stuffy confines of the train. The wire from his uncle said he would be at the station when Clay arrived. Across the platform, Clay noticed a middle-aged couple eyeing each passenger as they disembarked. They had to be Gary and Clara Tyler.

"Clay," the man exclaimed, hurrying across the platform. "I would have known you anywhere. You look so much like your namesake its uncanny. It's as though the years have melted away, and my brother is standing in front of me again. I'm your Uncle Gary."

"Don't smother the boy, dear," the woman admonished. "It's a long trip. Remember how it exhausted Jesse."

At the mention of his mother's name, unmanly tears prickled against the back of Clay's eyes. Other than the softness in his uncle's voice when he spoke of someone Clay resembled, nothing else gave a clue they might be related. Clay stood stiffly as these strangers embraced him.

"You're younger than my son Eli, but I'm certain you'll be great friends. Have you ever worked on a farm?"

"There's not much farming around Virginia City, sir," Clay replied. "I did spend last summer working at the assay office. Ma was against it, but Pa said it would do me good to get my hands dirty."

"Did you like it?"

"Not really. I'm studying to be a doctor. Dirt and medicine don't go together."

Across the way, Clay noticed the telegraph office. Somehow, he would have to disengage tactfully from these strangers who claimed to be his family, so he could send a wire to Ellie and let her know he'd arrived.

The look on his uncle's face when he mentioned getting dirty told him this wasn't a man he should cross. What was it the dime novel said about him? Oh yes, gentle—and yet he was the one who threatened to shoot his brother in the back to save his sister's life. How would he react to a nephew whose background was completely different from his own?

"Don't keep the boy out here all day, Gary," Clara said, reaching for Clay's hand. "You come along with me. My husband would talk your ear off if I'd let him. If I'm not mistaken you've got folks back in Virginia City who will be worried about you."

"Yes, ma'am."

"I won't have you calling me that. I'm your Aunt Clara. You don't know how long I've waited to hear one of Jesse's children call me that. Gary will see to your bags."

Clay glanced back at his uncle. The man's expression had turned from disapproving to a broad smile. Apparently, his aunt could turn his uncle from unrelenting to putty in her hands.

Clay followed her into the telegraph office, mentally composing the wire he would send to Jason. It would do no good to send one to Ellie. She hadn't left the house since the funeral. By rights, he should have stayed by her side, but his curiosity about his family's past overshadowed his sense of duty to Ellie. Jason and Sam would protect his sister, and Sally would be her companion.

The telegraph office was in a building adjacent to the train station. It was evident the operator maintained living quarters there as well.

To Clay's surprise, two women were at the desk. The old one looked very much like any other woman of her generation. Her brown hair was braided and coiled neatly around her head. She wore a dark suit, even though she must have been sweltering in the noonday heat.

The younger of the two was evidently the daughter. Her hair was a soft honey blond and had been cut in a fashionable bob like the girls at school wore. Her crisp white blouse had short sleeves and was open enough at the neckline to give Clay a hint of her high set breasts. She was definitely someone he wanted to get to know during his stay in Loveland.

"Good afternoon, Mrs. Tyler," the older woman greeted them as soon as they approached the counter.

"Good afternoon to you, too. Della, I *do* wish you'd call me Clara though. This is my nephew, Clay Martin."

"We feel like we know you already, don't we, Mama?" the younger woman observed. "I'm Amy Baines. I've been delivering your telegrams out to Mr. Tyler. It's a real pleasure."

She held out her hand, and Clay was surprised by her firm handshake. The woman Aunt Clara called Della merely smiled and nodded. It was evident she didn't appreciate her daughter's behavior.

"He won't bite, Mama," Amy continued.

Della finally extended her hand as well. "It's a pleasure to get to meet you, Mr. Martin. Being in the business we are, my daughter and I know more about folks than we should. That doesn't mean we're prone to gossip. I'm certain Mr. and Mrs.—I mean Gary and Clara—are looking forward to having you with them this summer. I am sorry about the loss of your parents.

Clay thanked the woman. She certainly wasn't native to this town, nor was she a farmer's daughter. Her speech was too refined for one with a country education. He'd learned to tell the difference at school. The daughter, on the other hand, hadn't received the same benefits.

For a moment he'd become so engrossed by the two women, Clay almost forgot his reason for being there. In front of him sat a pad and a pencil. Without further hesitation, he picked them up and wrote down his message.

JASON—ARRIVED SAFELY—HOPE ALL IS WELL WITH YOU
—CLAY

He handed the message back to the younger woman along with two dollars.

"That far too much, Mr. Martin," Amy protested.

Clay waved away her argument. "I'm certain you've earned that and more with the number of wires we've been sending lately. Oh, another thing, the name is Clay. I answer to that sooner than I ever would to mister."

"Once Clay gets settled, Gary wants to have a party to introduce him around," Clara said, her statement surprising Clay. "I *do* hope there is someone who can relieve you and Amy so you can both attend, Della."

"I'm not sure, Clara. Even if I am unable to attend, it will do Amy a world of good to have an evening out."

Clay watched his aunt nod her approval and then followed her from the office. He wondered if he caught a hint of a matchmaker's suggestion in her tone of voice. It certainly wasn't hard to recognize. He'd heard it from his mother enough times.

"Gary promised to take us to lunch at the café, and then we'll go out to the farm."

Clay nodded. As they walked down the sidewalk, he looked for his aunt and uncle's car. To his amazement, the only things he saw on the street were assorted farm wagons and a horse and carriage.

"Don't you have an automobile?" Clay said, once Gary joined them and they'd placed their order.

"Can't see the need. Don't tell me your mother approved of such nonsense."

Clay laughed. "You sound just like her. She fought Pa and Jason tooth and nail about getting one, but she finally gave in."

"Funny, I can't imagine Jesse without a horse."

A lump formed in Clay's throat. He quickly swallowed it before continuing. "I never saw Ma sit a horse. Pa told stories about how she could ride, but we never saw it. Of course, the book I found about her riding with you and the gang said she was an expert horsewoman."

To Clay's surprise, Gary's smile faded and his features hardened. "That book said a lot of things, most of them didn't have an ounce of truth to them. The one thing that did was about the way your ma handled herself on a horse. Our pa told her she was to be as good with a gun as your namesake, Clay, as good with the horses as me, and as ruthless as Frank."

Clay stared at his uncle in disbelief. Even though his pa told him about how his ma could ride a horse, he'd found it hard to believe. Even harder to believe was his sweet, meek, little mother handling a gun.

"Are you sure you're talking about my mother?"

The smile reappeared on Gary's face. "She was pure poetry in motion. After the first weeks on the trail, she never missed the target and rode like one of those women you see in the Wild West shows."

Before Clay could comment further, the waitress brought their food. "This must be your nephew, Mr. Tyler," she remarked. "I've heard a lot of talk about him coming to town. I'm pleased to meet you. My name is Mary."

The way the girl batted her eyes it was clear she was flirting. Whether she wanted a bigger tip or something in a more personal level later, Clay knew she was wasting her time. Things might have been different if the girl doing the flirting had been Amy.

* * * *

"Are you going to send that wire, or just sit there staring out the window and chewing on your pencil?"

Amy turned at her mother's question. She had to admit, Clay Martin was the most intriguing man who ever came through Loveland.

"He's not for you."

"Why not?" Amy countered. "What's wrong with me?"

Della didn't answer Amy's question. Instead, she clucked her tongue, a disapproving gesture she used to put Amy in her place. With that one gesture, a spanking had never been necessary.

Still thinking about Clay Martin, Amy began transmitting the words he'd printed to a series of key clicks. As she did, she tried to remember her father. He'd been gone for fifteen years and she had trouble remembering him. If it weren't for the picture her mother kept on the dresser, she would not know man who gave her life.

Thinking of her father brought her grandfather to mind. No matter how many years passed, she would never forget that man's face, the sound of his voice, or the words he spoke when he kicked them out of the only home she'd ever known.

"My son may have been taken in by your charms. He may have believed you when you told him your child belonged to him, but I'm not blinded by your Jezebel ways. Get out of my home and take your child with you. I don't care what you do or where you go, but don't ever consider trying to take any of my money."

Chapter Four

After his Aunt Clara insisted on sitting in the second seat to 'enjoy' the ride back to the farm, Clay climbed onto the front seat of the carriage next to his Uncle Gary. The earlier breeze he thought to be cool picked up and dark clouds threatened rain. Knowing the ride could become uncomfortable, he once again questioned the prudence of not having a closed automobile.

"Looks like we're going to get some rain," Gary said. "We sure could use it for this year's crops."

Clay agreed, but really didn't understand the need his uncle seemed to anticipate. The crops looked good to him. It certainly wasn't a desert as he'd heard the southern part of Nevada described. Of course, living in the mountainous area surrounding Virginia City, it wasn't rain that worried anyone. It was the depth of the winter snows.

"You were right when you said you weren't a farmer," Gary observed. "Around here rain is a gift from God. Things look good now, but if rain doesn't come on a regular basis, we could be in trouble almost overnight. Give it a few weeks and you'll see what I mean."

Clay looked skeptically at the darkening sky. "Rain is a necessary evil, but don't you worry about getting wet?"

Gary laughed. "To be truthful, neither Clara nor I will melt, but today we won't have to worry about it. That's the farm on your right. We'll be in the house before the storm hits."

"If I were home, I'd be able to read the signs better. Jason's bodyguard taught me about weather and the signs when I was a kid."

"That's one subject I want to talk to you about this summer. For now, let's get your aunt into the house before it starts raining."

Clay grabbed his bag from the back as Gary helped Clara down from the carriage. As Clay stepped onto the porch, he saw Gary leading the horse toward the barn.

"He'll be back soon," Clara said, drawing Clay's attention back to her.

"What's he doing?"

"He needs to get the horse unhitched and the carriage put away. He takes good care of his horses."

"Doesn't he have someone to do that for him?"

"Oh, Clay, you have so much to learn. Our life here is very simple. I can only imagine the kind of life you lead in Virginia City."

"Ma always had help, but it was because she was crippled. Pa always said it was his privilege to pamper her."

"I can imagine Russ saying something like that," Gary said from behind them.

Clay turned, surprised to see his uncle back so quickly. "I thought you were taking care of the horse."

"I ran into Eli at the barn, and he said I should come up to spend some time with you. Did I hear you right? Did your father actually have people to take care of his horses?"

"At first it was Jason's idea. When Pa's job got so demanding, it was almost mandatory. Sam suggested one of the Indian boys from the orphanage. One of the things I learned was Ma supported the orphanage while she worked at Jason's club and after she and Pa were married. The boy took great care of our horses and was eager to learn how to keep the automobile running as well. Pa sent him to school in Carson City. Thank goodness, he knew what he was doing. Ellie's going to need all the help she can get."

"I wonder if I would have even recognized my sister," Gary said.

Clay knew what he was talking about. The Jesse Martin he called Ma was probably closer to Laurel Morgan than she could ever be to Jesse Tyler. Somehow, he couldn't envision his mother doing any of the things the dime novel attributed to her. She was far too delicate to ride for long distances or camp out in the open.

"I doubt if you would have either," Clay agreed. "Like I told you earlier, I have read the book written about your family. I agree with you about not thinking much of it is true. I could never see my mother doing any of the things they attributed to her. She was far too fragile to sleep outdoors or be on the run for days on end."

Gary nodded sadly. "There is so much you don't know about your mother."

"And you have an entire summer to tell Clay about Jesse," Clara interrupted. "For now I'm sure he'd like to rest while Becky and I work on supper. Why don't you take Clay up to his room while I do?"

Clay watched, as once again Clara was able to calm Gary down and bring a smile to his lips.

"Your aunt is right. You've had a long trip, and I'm sure you'd like to clean up and get some rest. Just follow me."

Clay picked up his bag and went upstairs to a room with its windows facing south. Even with the falling rain, the entire room was far from gloomy. He could only imagine coming in here on a bright sunny day.

"This was our daughter's room. Of course, she's married and living in Peoria now." Clay saw a slight smile cross Gary's lips. "It was originally the room I used when I came here as a hired man."

Clay thought back to the book he'd read about the infamous Tyler gang. From it, he'd learned how Gary came to this farm rather than going to prison for his crimes. To look at the man today, no one would ever suspect this old farmer ever lived a life different from the one he lived now.

* * * *

Clay never thought he'd fall asleep when he first stretched out on the bed. To his surprise, he awoke to the aroma of fried chicken and the realization the rain had stopped. The sun also seemed to have moved almost to the western horizon indicating it was late in the afternoon.

He wondered what it was like to come to this farm as little more than a condemned man. The thought briefly crossing his mind came as a surprise. He hadn't wanted to believe what the novelist wrote about his family, but Gary confirmed at least the part about him working here as a hired man.

He noticed a washstand and pitcher in one corner of the room.

23

Rather than snoop around the unfamiliar house for a bathroom, he poured water from the pitcher to the bowl to wash for supper.

A tap at his door came just as he was drying his hands and face. "Yes," he said, opening the door to a young man with a strong resemblance to Clara.

"I'm your cousin, Eli," he said, extending his right hand. "Ma sent me up to get you for supper."

Clay shook his cousin's hand. "I'm Clay. Of course, I suppose you already know that. I was just getting ready to come down. Just so I know, where's the bathroom?"

Eli gave him a strange look. "The outhouse is just outside the back door. If you're used to indoor plumbing, I'm afraid you're out of luck. I've been trying to talk Pa into changing with the times, but he's stubborn."

Clay nodded. He knew about stubborn parents. If it hadn't been for Jason, his own parents wouldn't have updated their house or purchased an automobile.

"I understand. Just point me to the outhouse and I'll be ready for supper."

As soon as Clay returned to the kitchen, Clara dipped water from the reservoir in the cook stove to a pan so Clay could wash his hands with lye soap before eating.

Once he sat at the table, Eli introduced Clay to Becky, the woman who'd become his bride just a year earlier. The doctor in Clay soon realized the Missouri branch of his family would be increasing.

"It's too bad you won't be able to meet my sister Laura, but she and her husband live in Peoria, Illinois, and she's going to have a baby in September, so she isn't able to travel. I can understand why her husband is so protective of her because Becky is going to have a baby in November. I just wouldn't want either of them traveling in such a delicate condition."

Clay did his best to suppress his smile. The thought of pregnant women not being able to travel was no longer suggested. From what he'd learned in school, they were doing something very natural but they certainly weren't sick. How many of the women who settled this country were pampered when they gave birth?

With Gary seated to his right and Eli to his left, Clay was ready to reach for the platter of chicken when Gary grabbed one hand and Eli the other. A glance around the table told Clay Gary was about to say grace. Obediently he bowed his head while Gary began to thank God for the meal, Clay's safe arrival at the farm, and the afternoon's rainstorm.

"You do say grace at home, don't you?" Gary said as they began to eat.

"Yes sir, we do at home. Ma and Pa insisted on it. At school, it's another thing. We don't have many sit-down meals like this one. Sometimes I get something to eat in the dining hall and take it back to my dorm room so I can study. It's good to be doing something normal." He hoped his explanation appeased his uncle.

Gary ate in silence for a moment before turning back to Clay. "Then your mother didn't lose her faith again."

The word 'again' echoed in Clay's mind. "I don't think I know what you're talking about. Ma never ... did she?"

"That's not a proper story for table conversation, Gary," Clara admonished. "Why don't you tell us more about your mother, Clay?"

At first, Clay shook his head. Before the day of the funeral, he could have said any number of good things about his mother. Now with the story Jason told him when they returned home from the cemetery, he wasn't certain he ever knew his mother.

"I'm sorry to have asked such a sensitive question," Clara said, reaching across the table to touch Clay's hand.

"It's all right, Aunt Clara. My ma was the most gentle, fragile woman in the world. She had a personal maid, a cook, a groom, and a man to drive her automobile. I always knew we were rich, but I never knew where the money came from. After reading the book Jason gave me, I'm beginning to wonder if it could be part of the money taken from the robberies. If that's the case ..."

Gary's laughter interrupted Clay. The man was laughing so hard, he had to take off his spectacles and wipe his eyes with a red bandanna handkerchief. "It's true, we did steal a lot of money," he said once he regained his composure. "Through the spring and summer and even into the fall we'd pull of jobs in several towns. For the winter, we'd go down to Mexico where Pa and Frank would spend most of it on women and whiskey. Jesse and I never saw a penny of it.

"If her money came from anywhere, it was what she earned as Laurel Morgan or received as gifts from her admirers. I do know Jason Bellinger loved her enough to urge your father to marry her. He never deluded himself as to where her feelings lay. From what your father told me, Jason built the house for them while they were on their wedding trip."

Clay needed a moment to clear his mind. Jason was a good friend to both his parents. It couldn't be possible he had romantic feelings for Clay's mother.

"Pa worked hard. I haven't given any thought to the money that financed our lifestyle. I suppose it was because I never knew anything different."

Gary seemed to accept the explanation, and the table conversation turned to more neutral subjects. Nevertheless, Clay didn't let go of the subject of his parent's wealth. Growing up, it had been an accepted fact. They lived a life of luxury, which included servants as well as a college education without worry about the cost. Even with all of this, he'd been no different from any of the other children in Virginia City. He went to the same school and church as the Indian children from the orphanage. If he'd known of his mother's past, would any of it have been different?

"Why don't we go outside while the women clean up the kitchen?" Gary suggested, bringing Clay back into the conversation.

Clay looked at the two women who were already clearing the table. He hoped his uncle wouldn't ask him about any of the table conversation. To his surprise, Eli stood alone on the porch, smoking a cigarette.

"Where's Uncle Gary?" Clay asked.

"He's out in the barn checking on things. Even though I do most of the evening chores nowadays, Pa likes to make sure it's right. Most nights I go with him, but he thought I'd like to have some time to get to know you. Is it true you didn't know anything about the gang until your ma died?"

Clay nodded. "You don't buy all that outlaw stuff, do you? I read that book and ..."

"And nothing. I know Pa says there's not a lot of truth in it, but I've

26

heard his stories. I don't even want to think about living that way as a kid."

"I just can't imagine my mother ..."

"Imagine it. Your mother lived through hell just like my old man did. Tomorrow we'll go into town and visit the cemetery. Once you see the graves of Grandpa Tyler and Uncle Frank, maybe then you'll understand more. You do ride, don't you?"

Clay thought about Gary saying he wouldn't have an automobile. "It depends on the horse. Pa made sure I was riding almost before I could walk. I might be a little rusty, though. I haven't done much riding since I went to San Francisco to school, but it's something you don't forget."

Eli slapped him on the back. "For the first time you really do sound like a Tyler."

"It will take me a while to get used to that. I hadn't even heard the name Tyler until Ma died. I wish I had. Maybe it would have given me an excuse to let loose a little more when I was a kid. Ma and Pa always expected more out of me than any of my friends. What about you, were you a wild kid?"

"With my old man, there's no way. He's worked hard to overcome the past. Even if I wanted to act up on Saturday night, come Sunday morning Pa had me going to church. I remember once when Becky's brother, Paul, thought we should rob the general store to get some cigarettes. Becky's Pa found out what we were planning and hightailed it over here to talk to Pa. Needless to say the two of us worked our tails off that summer. After that, we decided it just wasn't worth the trouble. There's nothing anyone gets without working for it."

Clay understood completely. He remembered being a kid and wanting to do the things the other kids were doing. He'd gotten hold of a bottle of booze. Before he could get roaring drunk, his father caught him. He said it was never good to drink alone. Between the two of them they finished off the bottle, although Clay now knew he drank far more of it than his father. That evening and the next day, he'd paid the price of not only being sick but having to deal with the hangover. Even now, the thought of taking a drink of whiskey made him physically sick.

Chapter Five

Amy sat at the counter working on the books for the telegraph office. With more and more people in the area getting the new telephones, she wondered how much longer this job would be a necessity.

The tapping of the telegraph key denoted a new message. Since her mother was busy in the back, Amy grabbed a pad and pencil to take down the words being spelled out.

At the end of the message, she smiled, pleased to be able to go out to the Tyler farm to deliver it to Clay Martin. She was ready to go back and tell her mother of her plans when someone entered the office. A smile crossed her lips as she recognized Eli and Clay.

"Hi Amy," Eli said, taking off his hat. "I'm here on a mission for Ma and Becky. We're having a party on Saturday for Clay. You and your ma are invited to come."

"Your mother told us about the party yesterday," Della said from behind Amy. "I'm certain Amy will be there, but parties are for the young, and someone has to stay behind to take any incoming wires."

The mention of wires reminded Amy of the one she'd just taken for Clay. "Oh yes, I was about to take this wire out to the farm for you Mr. Martin."

"To begin with the name is Clay and I'm glad to have saved you a trip. Hopefully you won't have to make the trip out to the farm on business too many more times."

Amy prayed he was wrong. Time away from the office came as more than a welcome rescue from the day-to-day business of working with her mother. Without saying a word, she handed the envelope with the wire she'd just taken to Clay.

"Good news?" Eli said.

"It's from Jason," Clay replied after reading the message. "He says Ellie is coming around, and he's glad I got here all right. No need to reply, though. They both know I'm planning to spend the summer. Before I left, Jason told me if Ellie was up to it, he'd try to persuade her to come out and meet everyone later." Clay reached into his pocket and Amy knew he was going to offer her a tip.

"Oh no," she said. "That's not necessary. The wire was paid for on the other end and I didn't have to deliver it."

Clay smiled broadly. "You took your time to take the message. You deserve to be paid for what you do."

"My daughter is right," Della said, pushing the coins back across the counter toward Clay.

"It seems to me I'm the customer and the customer is always right." He winked broadly. "I'm looking forward to seeing you on Saturday. I'd be honored to come into town to pick you up."

"Oh, that won't be necessary," Amy protested. "I know my way out to the farm. You're the guest of honor. You need to be there. I'll see you on Saturday."

Amy watched as Clay and Eli left the office and walked down the street. She'd only heard about parties at the Tyler farm in the past. Having never been allowed to attend, she could only imagine there would be dancing, and she could almost feel Clay's arm around her waist as they danced.

"Don't think beyond your station, Amy," her mother admonished. "You know parties like the one the Tyler's are planning are not for you."

"Why not?" Amy argued. "Is it because we work for a living or do you think you're too good to work with the people of this town considering we came here from St. Louis?"

The look on Della's face was one of pure frustration. "You don't understand Amy. Don't you remember what your grandfather said about me? It's best if we keep our distance. I never want to hear those words again. As for this party, I think it's best if neither of us is there. We don't need bad words from these people. I'm too old to have to start over again."

* * * *

"Are you sure your sister is going to be all right?" Eli said, as they left the telegraph office.

"She's a strong person. Something tells me Ma's maid, Sally, won't put up with her pouting. I can just about hear her telling Ellie she needs to get her tail out of bed."

"She'd do that?" Eli inquired his eyebrows arched in surprise.

"You have to know Sally. When we were kids, Ma couldn't always run after us. More than once Sally gave me a swat on my bottom and told me what to do. She was always a second mother to us. If anyone can get Ellie out of bed it's Sally."

They walked away from the railway station, but Clay wasn't concentrating on their direction. "Do you think she'd come?"

"Who are you talking about?" Eli grinned.

"Amy of course. Do you think she'll come to the party on Saturday?"

"You've got it bad for her, don't you? I think she wants to come, but her mother is an old rip. I've known them ever since they came to town and the only thing Amy's ever gotten to do was work and go to school."

"Do you know why?"

Eli shook his head. "Not for sure. Amy was just a kid when Della moved here. I heard they came from St. Louis. It's all been very secretive, but Della rarely leaves the telegraph office. She's never been very sociable even though everyone has tried to get close to her. They don't even come to church and that really gets Pa going."

Clay thought about what Eli said. Silently, he wondered what his uncle would think if he knew medicine and science had often overridden organized religion in his life. Sunday morning easily became the one day when sleep overcame spiritual duty. Even his parents had no idea how lax he'd become when it came to going to church.

He walked side by side with Eli not really knowing where they were going until they finally stopped in front of two headstones in the cemetery. "Hanged for murder - April 16, 1888," Clay said, hardly able to get the words past his lips. "It's true, isn't it? Our grandfather was a monster."

"I know seeing this would have an impact on you. Caleb was bad but Frank was even worse. They used the other brothers like pawns in a sick game. Being the youngest Pa and Jesse took the brunt of everything. By the time Caleb went to get your Ma, Clay and Will were the only brothers other than Pa left. Jesse panicked on the first and only job she went on and Will was killed outright. Clay ended up being wounded and later swung from a rope."

Clay could feel a constricting of his throat as though a rough hemp rope was pulling tight, threatening to break his neck with one wrong move.

"Let's get out of here, Cousin. You're not looking so hot."

"It's ... it's just all of this is so new to me. I didn't expect to see proof of it all immortalized in stone. I don't believe in ghosts, but I wouldn't be surprised to see old Caleb coming out of his grave to get me."

"I used to have nightmares about him, but not as a ghost. I grew up on Pa's stories. There's not a ghost in the world that can hold a candle to them for being able to scare a kid half out of his mind."

From the cemetery, Eli headed back into town, leaving Clay to wonder where they were going.

"This is the sheriff's office and the jail where Caleb, Frank, and even my pa were held when your dad was the sheriff here." Eli held open the door so Clay could enter the small office.

"Got someone here you should meet," Eli said to the man sitting behind the desk. "Matt Langford, this is my cousin, Clay Martin."

"Russ' son?" The man rose to his feet. "I was just a kid when Russ was the sheriff here. The man's a legend in this town. It's a pleasure to meet you. How is your dad?"

"Uncle Russ as well as Aunt Jesse passed away last month," Eli said, as though he knew Clay would have trouble getting out the proper words.

Clay extended his hand, marveling at the small office once belonging to his father. In no way could it compare to the spacious office he had in Carson City. Even the office he maintained in their home was larger than this one.

"Russ was the reason I went into law enforcement. To hear the old timers talk about him, you'd swear he was the reincarnation of all the great lawmen of all times."

Clay nodded his acknowledgement before going back to the room housing the cells. Three small areas, resembling the animal cages he'd seen at the circus in San Francisco last fall, filled the enclosure. He tried to envision his Uncle Gary, who seemed so at home on the farm, caged here like an animal.

"How did your pa stand being in here?" Clay looked to Eli.

"I've asked him the same thing myself. He told me at the time he knew he was facing a rope. Even though he never killed anyone, Caleb had him, as well as your mother, believing if they were ever captured, they'd be hanged whether innocent or guilty. For proof of what he told them, he used the story of your namesake. They all knew he'd been hanged after he was captured. Pa said, at that point it didn't matter where they kept him. At least he was alive."

"Was my mother ever here?"

A look of surprise reflected from Eli's eyes. "You really don't have a clue about any of this, do you? Your mother was never on any wanted posters. Your dad went to watch Clay hang, that's when he first heard Jesse's name. He never expected to meet her face to face, much less fall in love with her. To be truthful, the story of the way they fell in love is one of the most beautiful tales of what things were like in the 'old' days."

Clay longed to be able to talk to his parents again. After this summer, maybe he'd be better prepared to ask Jason what more he knew about the family history.

"There's one more place I want you to see," Eli said, tugging on Clay's sleeve. "The building that housed your mother's seamstress shop is just down the street."

Reluctantly, Clay left the sheriff's office with its three-cell jail and echoes of the past ringing in his ears. A light breeze cleared the stink of the jail from his nostrils. To his right, he noticed a small house with a sign in front reading NETTIE'S NEEDLE.

"This was your mother's shop as well as her home until ..." Eli let the last of the sentence trail off unsaid.

"My mother actually ran this shop?" He stared at the neat place.

Eli nodded. "When she first came back to Loveland, it was her dream. She made the dresses for Ma and Pa's wedding and was working on her own wedding dress when Caleb and Frank came here to find her. Nettie Adams reopened the shop about ten years ago. She was just a kid when Jesse ran the shop, but she remembered what it was like before. That's when she bought the building and started her own place. She used the picture from the cover of the book and had a local artist do a portrait of Jesse."

Eli opened the door and a bell above it jangled merrily. Clay was glad Eli told him about the portrait. As soon as he saw it, he could almost feel his mother's love surrounding him.

"Hi Eli," the woman seated by the window to get the most benefit from the afternoon sunlight greeted them. "I heard you were in town."

Clay watched as Eli pulled yet another envelope from his pocket. "Becky and Ma are having a party on Saturday, so today I'm the delivery boy. I also wanted to introduce you to my cousin, Clay Martin."

Once again, Clay held out his hand in greeting and watched as a wide smile filled the woman's face. "I didn't know Jesse had a son. How is your mother?"

As it had at the Sheriff's office, a lump formed in Clay's throat at the mention of his mother's name. This time he regained his composure. "She and Pa both passed away last month. Thank you for asking, though."

A tear in Nettie's eye replaced the smile. "She was always frail. I remember coming here as a child. She was so kind. My ma died when she gave birth to my baby brother. It was Jesse who taught me how to sew. That was over thirty years ago, but whenever I step into this shop, I feel like she's looking over my shoulder and guiding my fingers. I'm sorry for your loss."

Clay ran his hand over the sewing table, trying hard to feel his mother's presence in the room.

"Everything in here is just the way Jesse left it," Nettie said as though reading his thoughts. "When she left town, Russ refused to sell this house. Ten years ago, I contacted the bank about it. I always thought it was a shame for it to remain empty. Someone must have talked to Russ because two weeks later the deed was delivered with a note. It was from Jesse. If I would reopen the seamstress shop, everything inside as well as the building would be mine if I gave the banker a dollar."

"A dollar," Clay echoed.

"It made the deal legal. This has become not only my business but also my home. Like your mother, I live in the back."

"This was my life, once upon a time," Jesse's voice echoed in Clay's mind. "There are happy memories here, but also horrors beyond belief. Don't be like me. Embrace the good. Get to know Gary. He can make sense of all of this for you."

Clay shook his head quieting his mother's voice just as his knees threatened to buckle. Rather than embarrass himself, he concentrated on the portrait of his mother until his mind cleared.

"Do you do well here?" he finally managed to ask.

"Oh yes, very well, thank you. I'm using the skills your mother taught me. It's only natural for me to dedicate this shop to her. If you stick around this town long enough, you'll find Jesse Tyler Martin was well loved."

Clay thanked Nettie and left the shop.

"I thought you were going to lose it in there," Eli said, once they returned to where they'd left the horses.

"I thought I was too. I heard Ma's voice. More than anywhere else, I felt her presence. She was happy here, but it was a different Jesse than the one I knew all my life."

* * * *

Clay allowed his thoughts to dominate the entire ride from town to his uncle's farm. He'd always known his mother could sew, because she made clothes for both himself and his sister when they were young. As for her own clothes, he never saw her working on the beautiful dresses she wore. It was possible Jason had them sent to her or maybe the money they never questioned was used to purchase them.

Gary was waiting for them when they rode into the dooryard. "Did you take Clay to all the places you wanted him to see, Eli?"

"Not all, but after we stopped at Nettie's place, I didn't think he was up to much more sightseeing. I thought he was going to be sick when we were at the shop."

"The Jesse here isn't my mother, at least not the mother I always knew. I couldn't believe Nettie hasn't changed anything in the shop. I could feel my mother there with me."

Gary laughed. "That wouldn't be hard with the portrait of her hanging there big as life. The first time I saw it, I had some bad flashbacks. You're right about everything being the same, that is, except one thing. Come out to the barn. I have something there that belonged to Jesse."

Clay looked skeptically at his uncle. "What could you have possibly kept for so long?"

"You'll see."

In the barn, Gary led the way to the tack room. From the top shelf, he pulled an oilskin bag and handed it to Clay. The weight of the bag came as a bit of a surprise.

"Is ... is this what I think it is?" Clay stammered.

"It's your mother's gun. By right's, I'm not supposed to have it, but your father gave it to me to keep. Until you arrived, I never knew why I kept it. It's certainly a bitter reminder of the kind of life we both lived for so long."

Clay pulled the gun from the bag and ran his hand over the barrel, the steel feeling cold and menacing. The pearl handle with the raised 'T' for Tyler matched the description he'd read in the book about the gang perfectly.

"She ... she really carried this?"

Gary nodded. "Not only did she carry it, but she was a crack shot. The only time she ever used it against another human being was the day she shot Pa at the shop. That's what threw her over the edge. On the day Pa and Frank were hanged, she disappeared. It was years before we had word she was in Virginia City. I'll always be grateful to Becky's Uncle Quade for recognizing her and contacting us."

"I told you there was horror at that shop," his mother's voice said. "Now you know what it was. The gun belongs to you. I was always afraid you'd follow your father's footsteps. If you had, I would have told you about everything and insisted you come here to get it from Gary."

"Can you teach me how to use this?" Clay said.

"I wouldn't be much of a teacher. I couldn't hit the broadside of a barn. When I was supposed to be learning how to use a gun, my eyesight was so bad, I couldn't hit the target. I took a lot of beatings from Pa and Frank because I couldn't shoot. Now it doesn't matter. I haven't held a handgun and pointed it another person since the day Jesse shot Pa. Besides, in this day and age there's no reason for any law abiding citizen to carry a gun."

Chapter Six

Amy looked at her reflection in the mirror over her dresser. Although she knew her mother didn't approve, she applied the rouge she'd purchased at the general store. She also smoothed the skirt of her new dress. She'd ordered it from Nettie several weeks ago, but knew it was perfect for tonight's party.

She couldn't believe Ma was letting her go to the party tonight. She surveyed the difference a little paint and powder could make.

"She's not here," she heard her mother shout.

"Then where is she?" a man demanded. Although Amy listened, she couldn't recognize his voice. "We have a warrant for both of you. Now, one more time where is she?"

Amy didn't wait to hear her mother's response. She needed help and considering this afternoon's party, everyone would be at the Tyler farm. As quietly as possible, she slipped out the back. There was no time to saddle Molly. Instead, she put the bit in her mouth. After the bridal and reins were in place, she led Molly to the end of the back ally. She made it to the station platform and looked over her shoulder.

Even though she wasn't dressed for riding, she used the platform to get on Molly's back. Certain she wasn't being followed, she turned the horse toward the road leading to the Tyler farm.

With every step the horse took, Amy kept looking over her shoulder. As worried as she was about her mother, Amy knew two women against one and probably two men were not good odds.

Carriages and automobiles filled the yard as she approached. Her arrival caused quite a stir as people gathered around Molly. It was Clay who helped her dismount. As much as she wanted to relish the touch of his hands on her waist, she knew her mother's safety was more important.

"There's trouble at the telegraph office," she gasped.

"What's going on?" Matt Langford asked.

"I ... I was getting ready to leave, and I heard Ma shouting at someone. It was at least one man. He said he had a warrant for our arrest. I don't know what that could be about. We haven't done anything." She watched as several young men hurried to their horses, including the sheriff.

"Let's get you in the house," Becky said as Amy watched the men riding back to town.

"I ... I should see to Molly," Amy protested.

"Gary is taking care of her," Clara said, putting her arm around Amy's waist to guide her toward the house. Almost instantly, the other women surrounded her.

For the first time, Amy became aware of her appearance. Her new dress was dusty from the wild ride from town and her legs burned from the unaccustomed contact with Molly's sweaty abdomen as she clung on as though her life depended on it.

* * * *

By two in the afternoon, people from town were beginning to arrive at the farm. Clay enjoyed meeting everyone, but kept glancing toward the road in the hopes of seeing Amy again. Even though Eli told him it was possible Della wouldn't allow her daughter to come today, Clay hoped his cousin was wrong.

He was engaged in conversation with Nettie when he caught a glimpse of a dust cloud on the road. As he focused, he recognized Amy riding as though the hounds of hell were on her heels. To his surprise, she was riding bareback, her skirt hitched up over her knees.

"There's trouble at the telegraph office," she gasped, after he helped her down from the horse.

Clay immediately looked around to see Matt elbowing his way to where he stood with Amy. For a moment, he wondered why Amy came here instead of going to the sheriff's office. A sick feeling filled Clay's stomach as he realized he was the reason. Eli invited everyone, including Matt, leaving the sheriff's office with only one deputy at the most.

His inner musings blocked whatever else Amy said. As much as he wanted to stay and comfort her, Clay knew he needed to go with the other young men to find out what was happening in town.

The door to the telegraph office stood open and the click of the key tapping out a message no one could take could be heard from the street. Inside, the office was in shambles and Della was nowhere to be found.

"I found Della," Eli called from the back living quarters. "She's hurt pretty bad. We have to get Doc over here now."

Clay's heart pounded as he tried to remember if the doctor had been out at the farm. Someone rushed past him in what he assumed was the search for the doctor. Rather than staying in the office, Clay made his way back to the living quarters.

In the bedroom, Della lay on the bed, a bruise forming around her eye and a split lip oozed blood. The sleeve of her dress was torn and her partially exposed breast embarrassed him.

"Can you hear me?" Matt asked.

Della nodded her head.

"What happened here?"

"There were two of them. They said they were U.S. Marshals and had warrant for Amy and me," Della's voice was barely louder than a whisper. "When I told them she wasn't here, they started to hit me. Thank goodness she heard them and left before they started searching the house."

"You can talk to Della later, Matt."

Clay turned to see a young woman with a medical bag enter the room. He didn't remember being introduced to her either the day he came into town with Eli nor at today's party. It was evident she was the doctor for this town. Even though he studied with two women in San Francisco, he knew they had to work much harder for the respect of not only their fellow students but also the professors. He wondered how these farmers accepted a woman doctor in their midst.

"I need to examine Della without a room full of young roosters watching me. Now scat. Make yourselves useful by cleaning up that mess in the office. While you're at it, see if you can find someone who can take down those messages. I don't know how Della takes that tapping all hours of the day and night."

Clay followed the others back into the office. "I know Morse code," a man he recognized as Phil Kerns, the station manager said.

While everyone pitched in to start putting the office in order, Phil sat at the desk and wrote down the telegraph messages as they came.

"Can you send a wire for me?" Clay queried.

"Of course I can," Phil said, a little indignant.

Clay grabbed a pencil and paper to write out his message. "My pa was a U.S. Marshal. There should be an office in St. Louis. If the men who did this were Marshals, I should be able to find out what kind of warrants they might have out for Della and Amy."

Clay listened as Phil clicked the keys spelling out his message. He wondered what would have happened if Amy hadn't been able to get out of the house and come to the farm. Della was injured, but since the intruders didn't take her with them, therefore Amy was the reason they came to Loveland, but why?

It didn't take long for an answer to come across the wire. There were no warrants issued for either Della or Amy and no U.S. Marshals sent to anywhere in the area.

"I think this is something the Marshals should be investigating," Matt observed. "Can you send another message, Phil?"

"Just write out what you want."

"Are you going to ask them to send someone out here?" Clay said. "If so, I think I might know a Marshal there. Rex Flint worked with Pa for years before he transferred to St. Louis. It always helps to work with someone you know."

"I thought you were studying to become a doctor," Eli said. "Are you sure that's what you want to do?"

"Ever since I got that wire saying Pa had been shot and Ma was sick I don't know what I want or who I am. Why do you think I came here this summer? I had plans to be at home and spend time with my parents. The only way I can do that now is to go down to the cemetery. By coming here, I hope to find out more about my family. At this point, I don't care about anything in my life more than finding out who did something like this to Della and threatened Amy."

"I need a couple of you men to help me move Della over to my office," Dr. Addison said as entered the office. "She's got some broken ribs and a broken wrist. I can't bind her ribs here, and I certainly can't put a cast on her wrist. I also want her to stay at the hospital for a few days. I don't think she's going to be safe here."

Clay immediately followed the young woman into the bedroom. Della was asleep, probably from some drugs the doctor gave her for the pain.

"I'm studying to be a doctor," Clay said, hoping that information would tell Dr. Addison he could possibly be of help.

"I know you are. I heard you were coming here. I graduated from school in San Francisco the year you started your studies. Every young woman on campus was enamored with you. I heard your name bantered around quite a bit by my roommates. By the way, my first name is Marie, Mari, and I would appreciate any help you can give me."

"Is there anything you can't do?" Eli teased.

"I can't work the horses the way you can," Clay replied, "and I'm not much of a farmer. If Ma hadn't insisted I go to college to be a doctor, I probably would have asked Pa to get me a job with the Marshals. Of course, once I learned about my family, I doubt I would have been considered for that job either."

Reluctant to pick Della up and cause further damage, Clay, Eli, and two other men lifted the mattress off the bed and used it as a stretcher to carry her from the telegraph office to the bed of the wagon Marie brought over from her office.

"Do you know how to mix plaster for a cast?" Marie said, once Della rested comfortably in one of the beds of the hospital built on behind the house where Marie not only lived but also had her office.

Clay nodded, glad he'd done well in the class on setting broken bones last semester. He found the materials and began to prepare the plaster. As he worked, he marveled at the modern medical facility Marie had in this seemingly dated town. By the time he had the plaster for the cast ready, Marie finished taping Della's ribs.

"How did you ever end up in a place like Loveland?" Clay spoke as he helped to apply the cast.

"I came here with my husband after we graduated."

"Husband?" Clay wondered why he hadn't seen another doctor anywhere in the clinic.

"Doug took a patient to Kansas City to see a specialist. He should be back next week. We're lucky to be close to such a good facility."

Clay looked around for a second time. "You have a good place here. It's not what I expected."

"It was the same with us. Thank goodness it was all in place when we got here. The people in this town seem to like to hold onto the past, but they want up-to-date medical care."

A moan from the bed where Della lay drew their attention to the injured woman. "Amy!" she called. "Where's Amy?"

"Amy's safe," Clay assured her. "She's out at the Tyler farm with the other women. Do you have any idea who did this to you?"

Della slowly shook her head as she drifted back to sleep.

"She needs to rest," Marie advised. "I doubt there's anything else you can do for her. Why don't you go back to your party?"

Clay agreed. He did want to get back out to the farm to check on Amy and make sure she was all right.

* * * *

Amy looked into the mirror after cleaning up. The carefully applied paint and powder she'd put on earlier was now washed away and in its stead was the same old Amy. That was where the familiar gave way to the fright of earlier in the day. Her stockings were ripped, and her thighs rubbed raw from clinging to Molly's sides. Even her new dress had lost its crispness.

The one thing left intact was her life. Only she wasn't so sure about her mother. Although she begged all the older men at the party to take her back into town, they all refused, saying they weren't sure if it was safe to do so.

"They're back," Amy heard Becky call from the other room.

Putting aside any thoughts of her appearance, she hurried out to the front porch. As soon as she stepped outside, she scanned the group of riders, but couldn't find Clay.

Eli rode up to the house. After dismounting, he bounded up the steps and pulled Amy into an embrace and then held her at arm's length.

"Thank God you got out of there and didn't get hurt."

"Ma? What happened to Ma? Where's Clay?"

"When we got to the telegraph office, we found a terrible mess. I went back into your house and found your ma. She'd been beaten and has some broken bones. We got her over to the hospital, and Dr. Maria is taking care of her. Clay stayed behind to see if he could help."

"I have to go to her," Amy protested. As she did, Eli tightened his grip on her arms.

"Matt thinks it's best if you stay out here for a while. These men weren't Marshals, and they didn't arrest your ma. We've already contacted the U.S. Marshall's office in St. Louis. Since they have no agents in this area, they're sending someone out to investigate. In the meantime, Matt wants you to stay out here with us where you'll be safe."

"What about Ma? How safe will she be?"

"She'll be at the hospital, and Matt is posting a guard. When she's well enough to be released, we'll figure out where she'll be safe."

"What about the office? Who will be taking the wires?"

"Phil says between him and some of his employees they can handle it. What none of us can handle is anything more happening to either you or your ma."

Amy tried to put everything into perspective. She knew she should be concerned about her safety, but now she only wanted to be with her mother.

"Can I see her?" she finally managed to ask.

"Not tonight. I'm certain the doctor will keep her sedated at least until morning. For now, there's plenty of food, and the band is just getting warmed up. If you hadn't come out here, we wouldn't have found Della. You more than likely saved her life. Tomorrow morning will be soon enough. We'll go into town for church and then go over to the hospital."

The word church bothered Amy. In all the years they'd lived in Loveland, they'd never attended church. She'd asked her mother about it and was told Grandfather Baines went to church on Sunday, and if he was an example of being a Christian, she wanted nothing to do with it.

Amy was still deep in thought when Clay rode into the dooryard. As soon as she saw him, she hurried to his side to hear what he had to say about her mother.

"How is she?" Amy pleaded. "Is she ..."

As Eli did earlier, Clay pulled Amy into an embrace, silencing her before she could finish. "She's bruised around her face, but that's minor. She has several broken ribs that Doctor Marie wrapped, and she's encased Della's broken wrist. Marie assured me your ma will sleep until tomorrow.

Clay released his embrace and took Amy's arm to turn her toward the house. "Let's go into the house and get something to eat. I'm starving and you must be, too."

After filling their plates, they made their way to one of the tables dotting the lawn. Before long Matt joined them.

"What do you remember hearing before you came out here?" he said.

"I heard them tell Ma they had warrants for both of us, but they seemed to be interested in finding me."

"Do you know of any reason why someone would want to find you?" Matt pressed.

Amy thought for a moment. As she did, she remembered a wire her mother took several days earlier. Amy heard the click of the keys and put aside the bookwork so she could go out and deliver the wire.

"That bastard," she remembered her mother shouting. "How could he have found us? It's been so long. We should be safe by now."

Before Amy could look at the message, her mother crumpled the paper and threw it into the fire of the small stove used to heat the office.

"What did the wire say?" Amy watched her mother shake her head and refuse to say anything more.

"Did you hear me, Amy? Do you know of any reason why someone would want to find you?" Matt said for the second time.

"I'm sorry, Matt. I was trying to think of something," she said, knowing she'd just told the sheriff an out and out lie.

Before she could say anything more, she had to talk to her mother. If Grandfather Baines was looking for them, they could be in danger. From what she remembered of him, he was an angry old man who wanted them completely out of his life and perhaps even dead.

* * * *

Clay watched Amy's face intently as she talked to Matt. Something in her expression told him she wasn't being completely truthful with the sheriff. Maybe Amy's past was as mysterious and dark as his own.

From the other side of the yard, he heard the music begin. "Come on, Amy," he said. "There's nothing you can do for your mother tonight. Why don't you come out and dance with me?"

For the first time since Amy rode into the dooryard, she gave him a brilliant smile. "Why thank you, Mr. Martin. I'd be honored to be your partner."

Clay took her hand and led her to where people were dancing. Even though she allowed him to take her in his arms and spin her around to the beat of the music, he could tell she was far from relaxed. Whether it was her mother's condition or Matt's question that caused her tension, he intended to find out.

Chapter Seven

Clay woke to the morning activity of the farm. Rather than feeling rested, he was as tired as he'd been when he first went to bed the night before. Getting up was the last thing he wanted to do. Throughout the night, his dreams had been filled with the memories of what they'd found at the telegraph office.

Knowing so little about the outlaw gang his grandfather ran and his mother and uncles rode with, made him wonder if they were capable of being as brutal with their victims as the men who were looking for Amy and beat Della.

After washing, he made his way down to the kitchen for breakfast. Although he'd dressed in his Sunday suit, he already knew he wouldn't be going to church with the family. He was anxious to get to the hospital and check on Della. He had a lifetime of Sundays to go to church, but today the doctor in him needed to visit 'his' patient.

Where had that come from? Della was no more his patient than any of the people whose bedsides he'd stood at in training. Was it because he'd been the first medical person to see Della and assess her condition or was it because Della was Amy's mother?

Once he stepped into the kitchen, he noticed Amy dressed in something different from what she wore last night. It was evident she'd borrowed the dress from Becky because it hung loosely on Amy's smaller frame.

"As soon as we finish breakfast, we'll be leaving for church," Eli said once the obligatory table grace ended. "Clay and I can ride into town that is if Molly will allow at least one of us on her back. That way Pa can drive you girls in the carriage."

"I doubt either of you will have a problem with Molly," Amy replied. "I hope you'll understand why I won't be going to church with your family. Ma and me, well, we just don't go to church. There's always too much work to do and, to be truthful, it just isn't for us."

Clay noticed the look of disapproval on his uncle's face. It was evident Gary took going to church seriously.

"I guess there's no time like the present to tell you I won't be going to church either," he announced.

"Why not?" Gary demanded. "Do you mean to tell me you can't give a Sunday morning to the Lord?"

Clay could almost hear his father saying the same thing. "I have the rest of my life to go to church. I think God will understand my need to check on Della. I feel as though she's 'my' patient."

"Your patient will be there after church," Gary spat. "I can't believe your mother would accept such behavior from you. In this house ..."

"Calm down, Gary," Clara admonished. "I seem to remember an angry young man who refused to believe in God. I agree with Clay. You have to keep in mind Clay is studying to be a doctor. In a way, he will be doing God's work. Maybe you should go back and read your Bible. It seems to me Jesus healed the sick on the Sabbath."

Clay smiled at how, once again his aunt calmed his uncle's temper. Having never seen anyone become so angry, he wondered if his grandfather's temper influenced Gary more than anyone knew.

* * * *

Once in town, Clay and Amy walked the horses over to the telegraph office. With the tension seemingly lessened, everyone agreed it would be best if Clay stayed with Amy. It would be safer for her to return home and pack a bag with him at her side.

"You really don't have to stay with me," Amy protested. "I'm a big girl. I can take care of myself."

"I doubt that. You forget I saw the damage these men did to the place yesterday. I'm not the first one to tell you it's not safe for you to stay here alone."

They entered the office. Although things had been somewhat cleaned up the day before, the horrors of what happened were still evident. Amy's gasp of shock brought his mind back from the memory of what he'd seen here less than twenty-four hours earlier.

"Oh, Clay, this is terrible. Who could have come in here and done all this damage?"

Clay had no answer to give her. Unfortunately, in his gut he knew there was definitely something Amy wasn't telling Matt. He just didn't know what it was.

* * * *

Amy tried to block out the damage done to not only the office but also the living quarters she shared with her mother. Clay was right, she didn't want to stay here alone. After packing a bag to take out to the farm, she was ready to shut the door and come back another day when she felt up to the task.

"I think I have everything I need," she said when she reentered the office. To her surprise, Clay was busy cleaning up the mess the others had left unfinished. "You don't have to do this."

"I know I don't have to do this, but it was something to pass the time."

Amy smiled. "Maybe I should have told you to hitch Molly to the carriage instead."

Clay crossed the room to stand beside her. "I'm way ahead of you. I thought you'd be done by the time I finished, but I guess women take longer to pack things than men."

Amy glanced at the clock. How had so much time gotten away from her? "I ... I didn't mean to take so long I really do want to get over to see Ma."

"I know you do. Give me your bag, and we'll go over together."

Amy allowed Clay to take her hand. Behind her, she heard the click of the telegraph key and for the first time ignored it. Phil sat at the desk recording the message, letter by letter.

Clay helped her get into the carriage, then went around to the other side, and took the reins. Molly responded the way she always did when she pulled the carriage. Amy glanced back and saw the second horse tied to the back.

"It seems strange to think I won't be coming here for a while," she said half to herself.

"Haven't you ever been away from home before?" Clay said.

She was surprised to hear him question what she hardly voiced aloud. "Not really. I was very young when Ma brought me here so she could take this position. To be honest, we really don't socialize much. Ma says it's best this way because then no one can hold anything against us."

"So where did you call home before you came here?" Clay pressed as he snapped the reins to turn toward the hospital.

We lived in St. Louis until my father died. After that, Ma had to get a job so she could support us. Luckily, her father had worked in a telegraph office and taught her Morse code, just as she taught me. Even though she couldn't get a job in St. Louis, she did work as a maid. From her employer, she learned of the position here."

Clay made no further comment, but continued to drive to the hospital. The closer they got, the more anxious Amy grew. She knew she had to confront her mother, about the mysterious wire. It was most certainly a clue to what happened the day before.

* * * *

Clay thought about what Amy told him. With Della's skills he wondered why she would leave a city the size of St. Louis to move to a small town like Loveland.

As soon as they walked into the clinic, he saw Marie checking what he assumed to be Della's chart. "How's your patient this morning?"

Marie looked up and smiled. "She's not happy about being here and even more so when she learned Matt doesn't want her to go home."

"I can understand that," Amy said. "Can I go in and see her?"

"Of course you can. Let's give Amy and Della a moment alone, Clay. I'd like to talk to you in private."

Clay watched as Amy made her way to her mother's room. "Is something wrong?" he inquired once he was certain only she could hear him.

"To begin with, Della's not well. I found a mass in her stomach. I'm afraid it might be cancer. When I questioned her about it, she wasn't surprised. I'm afraid she doesn't have long to live. She's been putting on a good act, but this beating she took didn't make things better. The other thing I wanted to tell you is what she said in her sleep. The night nurse recorded this." She handed him the chart so he could read for himself what Della said in her ramblings.

You can't have Amy. She's mine. I won't allow you to taint her mind with your hurtful lies.

The note on the chart posed more questions without answers.

* * * *

Amy walked down the silent hall of the clinic until she came to the room where her mother rested. Without announcing her presence, she stood in the doorway and assessed the woman who represented her whole life. Who could have done this to Ma?

"Amy, oh Amy, is that really you? I'm not dreaming, am I? I was so afraid they'd find you."

Amy rushed to her mother's bedside. "Yes, Ma, it's me. I've been so worried about you. Who could have done something like this?"

"I'm afraid there's a lot you don't know about our lives."

"What don't I know?" Amy was concerned about what her mother said.

"There is so much, so very much," her mother replied, her voice sounding suddenly weak and old. "For now, the important thing you must know is that I'm dying. I've known I was sick for a long time. Dr. Marie confirmed my self-diagnosis. Unfortunately, the beating I took must have ruptured something inside me."

"No. You can't be sick."

"I can and I am. I don't have the strength to tell you the rest. It's all in my journal. Just promise me you won't read it until I'm gone. I've kept it all from you for the past fifteen years, and I can't stand to have you blaming me."

"Why would I blame you? It's always been the two of us against the world. You're not making any sense."

"I'm making more sense than you know. Just give me your word you won't do anything until I'm gone."

"I promise, Ma."

Before Della could say anything more, she closed her eyes and drifted off to sleep. The tears Amy refused to shed in front of her mother, cascaded down her cheeks. She refused to think about what she would find in her mother's journal. So many horrible things happened in the past two days she didn't know if she could stand another blow to shatter her life even further.

"Are you all right?" Clay, startled Amy.

She quickly wiped at her tears before turning to face him. "Ma says she's sick and she ... she's ..."

"I know. I talked to Marie, and she told me. I can't believe she was able to keep it from you for so long."

Amy wondered if she noticed a catch in Clay's voice. Since he was studying to be a doctor, wouldn't he be able to keep his emotions in check?

"It's hard to lose a parent," Clay continued when she said nothing "I should know. Just before I came to Loveland I lost both my mother and my father within hours of each other."

Amy remembered the wires she'd delivered to the Tyler farm weeks earlier. "Of course, you know how I feel about hearing this without any warning."

"I do. My mother had been in ill health for years, but Pa was totally unexpected."

He didn't elaborate further, and Amy knew better than to ask. Hearing the pain in his voice told her his father's passing was perhaps as horrible as what she was going through.

Together, they sat at Della's bedside until her breathing became slower and more labored. With each breath, Amy wished her mother would open her eyes and say one last thing to her, but at the same time, knew the end was at hand.

It seemed as though they sat in the room for hours, when the next breath didn't come. Clay was immediately on his feet checking for a pulse. He shook his head as he left the room to find Maria so she could confirm the time of death.

Amy's tears fell and her heart broke as she realized now she was completely alone in the world. She also wondered exactly what she would find in her mother's journal. Whatever it was she knew it would change her life forever.

Chapter Eight

The day after Della's passing, U.S. Marshal Rex Flint arrived on the afternoon train. He'd sent a wire before leaving St. Louis, so Clay hitched the team to the wagon and went to meet his train.

"Clay, it's good to see you," Flint said, shaking Clay's hand as soon as he got off the train. "I was sorry to hear about your parents. They were good people. What can you tell me about what's going on here?"

"Not much. Della Baines was assaulted in her office, and, unfortunately, she died shortly afterwards."

"Are we talking murder here?"

"Yes and no. I think her death was hastened by the beating, but she was very sick with cancer. I honestly don't know what to say about murder. That's your job as it was my father's. One way or another, she would have died, but the beating hastened it."

"Do you have any idea why anyone would do this?"

"Not really. From what I gathered from her daughter, Amy, I don't think they wanted Della as much as they did Amy. They kept asking Della where her daughter was."

Rex picked up his traveling bag and followed Clay to where he'd left the horse and wagon.

"What? No car?" Rex grinned.

"This is a farming community. Although some people in town have automobiles, my uncle raises horses and thinks cars are just a passing fancy."

"Ah yes. I've heard about your uncle. Back several years ago, there wasn't a lawman in the country who hadn't heard of the Tyler gang. Of course, that was way before my time, but your father told me the story when I worked with him in Virginia City. I've often wondered how you felt about growing up in the shadow of such an infamous family."

"To be truthful, I never knew about any of it until after my parents died. I'm having a hard time coming to grips with the thought of my mother being involved in such a life. She was just too frail."

"It's strange, those are the same words Russ used to describe Jesse. I checked into things and learned she was a crack shot, but never involved in the robberies and murders her father and brothers committed."

"I gathered as much when I visited the graves of my grandfather and Frank. Gary seems to be a decent sort though."

"So I've heard. I think he and your mother were very much alike. From what I've read about Gary's trial, he was nothing more than a pawn in his father's evil plan."

Clay took Rex to the hotel so he could talk to people in town and see if anyone knew anything about the attack on Della and the threat posed to Amy.

* * * *

The next few days were a blur for Amy. Gary and Eli were both insistent on having the funeral at the church rather than the graveside service Amy knew her mother would have wanted. For as long as she could remember, her mother had shunned the church and anything to do with it. Through her grief, though, she allowed the Tyler family to take over the planning of everything concerning the last thing she could do for her mother.

To her surprise, the church was filled with mourners from every walk of life in Loveland. Even officials from the railroad were in attendance. Everyone expressed their sympathy and promised to help her in any way possible. Even her job at the telegraph office was being held for her until she was mentally and physically able to return to work.

She felt safe to think Marshal Flint attended the funeral to make certain no one was there to do her harm.

The morning after the funeral, she hitched Molly to the carriage and went back to the home she shared with her mother to search for the journal. She was pleased when Clay insisted on going with her. She knew she definitely needed his support when she read the secret her mother told her she'd kept for the past fifteen years.

Once they arrived at the telegraph office, Marshal Flint met them. "I hope you don't mind if I come in with you," he said. "There's no telling if someone could be waiting for you to return."

Amy agreed. She didn't want to go into her former home alone and even Clay's presence didn't calm her fears. The Marshal would certainly be able to protect them.

"Do you have any idea where to look for the journal?" Clay said as they entered the living quarters behind the telegraph office.

"It's more than likely in the drawer of her bedside table. We both understood not to invade each other's space. She always told me anything I wanted to keep private I should put in the drawer next to my bed and she wouldn't ever look at it."

Going into her mother's bedroom, she hesitated as she put her hand on the pull of the drawer that had always been forbidden to her. For a moment, she felt like a child snooping in her mother's bedroom for something she shouldn't see. Finally she opened the drawer and saw the leather bound book she knew was the journal.

"Did you find it?" Clay said.

Amy could only nod. "I don't think I should read it here. Would you please take me back to the farm? Everyone there has been so kind to me, I want them with me when I find out what my mother hasn't been telling me."

"I think that's a good idea," Rex said. "Do you mind if I come along? It might shed some light on what's been happening."

"I'd like that, Marshal," Amy replied. "I used to think I was a strong person, but since last Saturday I'm afraid I'm little more than a frightened mouse."

* * * *

Clay took the black leather book Amy held out to him. He felt the same way as when Jason told him as well as Ellie about the life his mother once led. Was it possible Della Baines had as much of a criminal background as his mother and uncle?

The ride back to the farm was quiet as both he and Rex allowed

Amy time to think over what she might learn about her past once she read the journal her mother left as a legacy.

Once they were home, Clay assembled the family. "Amy wants us all to be here when she reads the journal her mother kept for years.

"I would appreciate it if you're read this," Amy said, handing Clay the envelope that preceded the handwritten journal.

Clay fingered the envelope before breaking the seal and taking out the sheets of paper contained within.

My Darling Amy,

There is so much I have not told you about our lives, but I am too much of a coward to tell you the truth, so if you are reading this letter, I am already gone.

To begin with our names are Darlene and Amanda Palter. I changed them after your father died, because of your grandfather and his threats to take you from me. Of course I'm ahead of myself.

I should start at the beginning. My father was a telegraph operator in St. Louis, but when he died, I was too young to take over his position. Besides, they wouldn't have hired a woman for the position, especially not a fifteen-year-old girl.

As for my mother, I know nothing of her. She married my father and when motherhood became too much for her, she abandoned us. Father had no recourse but to raise me the best way he knew.

When my father died, I knew I had to find employment since there was absolutely no money to support me. The only job I could find was cleaning houses, and I was lucky to find a position with Mrs. Palter. She was a wonderful woman, but unfortunately she was very ill and died shortly after hiring me.

In the months that followed, your father, James, came home from school and began courting me. Being young and without the guidance of a mother, I soon found myself pregnant. When your grandfather, Montgomery, found out, he kicked the both of us out of his house. We were allowed to live in the guesthouse on the property and were able to live off the inheritance James had from his mother.

It was two years later when your father became sick with consumption. He died a horrible death. The funeral was barely over when Montgomery told me to leave the house where we'd been living and if I tried to get any of his money, I would be charged with murder.

I tried to get a job at the telegraph office, but they told me there were no openings. I had no options but to go back to working as a maid in a prestigious home.

It didn't take Montgomery long to find me and insist I give him custody of you and never to see you again. At that time, I talked to my employer. He was very understanding, as he'd had business dealings with Montgomery and wanted only to help me. With his help, I learned of the position here in Loveland. We were able to change our names and move without telling anyone where we were going,

Through the years I've kept in contact with the wonderful man who made our new lives possible and learned of Montgomery's search for us. Until recently, he hadn't been successful in finding us.

A few days ago I received a telegram from my friend in St. Louis saying he'd heard Montgomery had finally been able to locate us and was planning to take you to St. Louis and into his household.

As I write this, I realize my days on this earth are limited and you should know who you really are. If Montgomery is intent on making you his heir, you will be a very wealthy young woman. Once I am gone you will be free to embrace the lifestyle he has to offer you, or you can continue to run from him and hope he never finds you. Whatever you decide to do, you know I love you and respect your wishes.

All I asked is that you don't judge me too harshly. I did only what I thought was in our best interest.

> *With All My Love,*
> *Mother*

"Montgomery Palter as in the shipping magnate?" Rex frowned.

Clay also recognized the name from things he'd heard while going to school in San Francisco. The man was a legend in the shipping industry even as far away as the West Coast.

"I ... I don't know. Do you think the men who came to the office and beat my mother were working for him? If so, he knows where to find me. I might as well change my name and move away. If he condones what happened to my mother, I want nothing to do with him."

"Don't be too hasty in your decision," Rex said. "I think you should at least meet the man. Your mother lived in fear of him for far too many years. I'm not saying she was wrong in running away, but this is the twentieth century. Men like him can't run roughshod over people like they could in the past. Let me do some research with my contacts in St.

Louis before you make any decisions."

Clay was disappointed when Eli volunteered to take Rex back to town. He'd wanted to pump Rex for any information he might have on Montgomery Palter and yet he also wanted to stay at Amy's side. Somehow, he couldn't think of her as Amanda. Unfortunately, even the duty of being with Amy had been taken from him. Becky and Clara insisted Amy should go upstairs to rest leaving Clay alone with Gary in the kitchen. At this point he felt as helpless as he had when he stood beside his father as he slipped from life to death.

"Why don't you come out to the barn with me?" Gary said, as he placed a consoling hand on Clay's shoulder. "I think it's time for you to learn more about the Tyler gang. Besides, there's nothing you can do in the house. Your Aunt Clara, as well as Becky, is taking good care of Amy."

Clay looked up and saw something in his uncle's eyes that somehow frightened him. What more was there to learn about his family than he'd already uncovered? Without making comment, he got to his feet and followed Gary out to the barn.

"You've heard some stories about the life your mother and I lived as teenagers. Although Jesse was older than I'd been when Pa first took me away, we both suffered at his hands. Your grandfather was an evil man. Three of my brothers lost their lives, and I never saw Pa grieve for any of them. He certainly beat my faith in God out of me. He tried to do the same with Jesse, but she wouldn't give up her faith."

"You said he beat you. How did he do it?"

"Pa and Frank were both good with a bullwhip."

Clay watched as Gary unbuttoned his shirt and removed it. Seeing the scars on his uncle's back made Clay sick to his stomach. More than anything else, he wanted to run away from the evidence of the violence his mother witnessed and endured in the years she should have been courted by young men and preparing for marriage.

"This has to be the reason Ma never told us about her past," he finally managed to say once he swallowed the gall rising from his stomach to his throat.

"I'm sure it is but that's not all of it. We thought our father was certain we were dead, but one day he came to Jesse's shop. She was preparing to marry your father and so very happy. When Pa and Frank came upon her, she pulled her gun and shot Pa."

Gary again pulled out the guns Clay saw days earlier. He remembered the weight of the one Gary said belonged to this mother and the horror of holding it in his hand. As much as he didn't want to see the reminder of the life his mother lead, he picked up the revolver once his uncle unwrapped it.

Even though he wanted nothing to do with this side of his mother's life, he knew it was important to acknowledge it. This gun and the matching one Gary now held were part of his family's past.

"These," Gary said, motioning to the guns, "were one of our gifts from Pa. The other was a price on our heads. Each of us had one and all of my brothers were good shots. All except me, that is. I took a lot of beatings because I couldn't shoot. Of course, later I learned it was my eyesight rather than my aim. Clay, your namesake, was the best shot of all of us. He never missed the target, and your mother was his equal."

"You said Ma shot your pa. She must not have killed him since the headstone in the cemetery says he was hanged."

"Your ma was scared to death of Pa and Frank, and it had been a long time since she'd shot her gun. Pa was wounded, but the worst damage was to Jesse's mind. After your pa arrested Caleb and Frank, she locked herself in the shop and that was the last time I saw her until Russ brought her back from Virginia City. The woman who returned was an elegant lady and not the sister I'd known all my life."

Clay thought of the story Jason told him about meeting Jesse on the riverboat and transforming her into Laurel Morgan. Just holding his mother's gun in his hands shattered every image of the woman he'd ever had. The Jesse he found here wasn't the frail elegant lady he equated with his mother. With what Gary just told him, she was little more than a frightened, beaten child.

Chapter Nine

The next morning Clay was surprised to see Rex at the front door to the farmhouse. "I've got some information regarding Montgomery Palter," he said as he came into the kitchen.

Clay watched as Amy held onto a chair for support. He knew the last few days had taken their toll on her. Since they read the letter from Della yesterday, she hadn't mentioned anything about its contents. He didn't even know if she'd read any of the entries in the journal.

"What about him?" Amy steadied herself.

"I wish I could tell you're your grandfather is a well-respected man, but what I've learned is he's mean spirited and also in poor health. The word is he's obsessed with his son's widow as well as his granddaughter, namely you. It's possible he wants to make amends before he dies."

"Well, he can die as the lonely old man he's been for the past fifteen years. I won't give him the satisfaction ..."

What she was saying was interrupted by the barking of the two dogs running loose in the yard. Before Gary could see what was bothering the dogs, someone began pounding on the door.

"Open up!" the voice of an angry sounding man shouted. "We know the girl is here. We have a warrant for her arrest."

Gary opened the door, and Clay gasped to see two men with guns drawn.

"Whoever you are, you aren't dealing with a helpless woman here," Gary said. "Why don't you put down your guns? Do you think this young lady is a dangerous criminal?"

The cold look in the eyes of the two men with their guns drawn told

Clay they could easily open fire. If the men didn't comply with his uncle's wishes more than one person in the room could lose their lives in the next moments.

"Get out of our way, old man. You have no idea who you're talking to. We're here to arrest Amy Baines, also known as Amanda Palter. You're interfering with two officers of the law. I'd just as soon as shoot everyone here then ..."

"Then what?" Rex demanded.

Clay glanced in Rex's direction and for the first time saw the gun the Marshal held in his hand.

"Who are you to be questioning us?" the second man insisted.

"I'm U.S. Marshal Rex Flint and, if you don't put down your guns and show me this so called warrant, I won't hesitate to pull the trigger on the gun I have under the table."

The men lowered their guns and started backing away from the door. Before they could get off the porch, Rex, Gary and Eli rushed out to tackle them.

Clay knew he should have joined his uncle and Eli, but years of living a quiet life in Virginia City as well as the hours spent in the classroom left him almost paralyzed with fear. He knew his father would have been as quick to act as Rex, but he wasn't his father.

By the time he got to his feet and stepped onto the porch, the two men were restrained. As though they'd been expecting trouble, Eli worked at tying them up with ropes.

Behind him Clay heard Clara and Becky trying to calm a sobbing Amy. Torn between the woman of whom he'd grown fond and his duty as a man, he stood on the porch watching the drama unfold.

"Now," Rex began, "who are you and what kind of warrant do you have for Miss Baines? I know you have no connection with the U.S. Marshal's Office in St. Louis."

The men glanced apprehensively from one to the other. "We're private investigators, from St. Louis. We're just following orders. We ain't done nothing wrong."

"You haven't? What do you call breaking into the telegraph office and beating an innocent woman, thus hastening her death?"

"That weren't us," the second man protested. "Our boss sent us out

61

here to take care of what the first two agents didn't and bring back the girl."

"Names," Rex demanded. "I want names. Who do you work for? Who ordered you to come to Loveland and seek out Miss Baines?"

"W ... we work for a private detective agency in St. Louis. We just follow orders. We were told to say we were U.S. Marshals, so the people holding the girl would hand her over to us. Our boss told us this was just a little backwater community and the rubes wouldn't know if we were what we said or not. He told us, people like that would believe anything."

"What's the name of this agency?" Clay demanded no longer able to hold his peace.

The man shook his head in denial.

"Like the man said, what is the name of this agency?" Rex reiterated Clay's question.

"That's none of your business," the second man spat.

Rex opened his jacket to display his Marshal's badge. "This badge makes it my business. Now, I'm asking again, what's the name of this agency?"

Clay had hear his father saying the same things. He knew he'd never make it in law enforcement. His temperament was better suited to medicine.

"We work for the Tampers Agency, but arresting us won't stop this. There are more agents that will be sent here to take our place when we don't get back to St. Louis."

Clay felt his chest tighten at the implication of what the man said.

"Gary and I will take these men into town to the jail," Rex said, breaking the tension of the situation. "Eli is hitching up a wagon, but I want the two of you to stay here with the women. If there are any other incidents, you'll be here to protect them."

Clay looked to his uncle for confirmation. Gary nodded. "The trip into town might not be anything either you or Eli should be party to."

Gary's statement confused Clay. By Gary going into town with Rex and leaving him and Eli behind, it was likely he expected more trouble.

"I won't know anything more until I contact my office in St. Louis," Rex added. "Once I know exactly what's going on I'll let you know. If I can believe these two, they're the second set of agents form their office sent out here. Whether they're right or not, I don't know, but I don't want to take any chances with Miss Baines' safety to say nothing of that of Clara and Becky."

Clay agreed, but he didn't completely understand. Virginia City was a mining town. Even though it could be rough and tough, he'd never been in fear for his or anyone else's safety.

"Maybe after this, Pa will finally consent to getting into the twentieth century," Eli said once Gary and Rex drove out of the yard with the two private investigators. "If he agreed to modernize this place, we'd have a telephone, and Rex would have had his answers without going into town."

"Don't get started on that again, Eli," Clara admonished. "The last thing we need out here is some machine on the wall interrupting our peace and quiet."

"I've heard all of this before. What if Rex finds out we're in danger? If we had a telephone, he could let us know right away. Since we won't know anything until Pa gets back, I've brought in Pa and Jesse's guns."

"You know how I feel about those guns," Clara cried.

"I agree with your ma," Becky said. "Those guns should stay in the barn where they belong. What if you shoot yourself or one of us?"

Clay watched as Eli rolled his eyes. As much as he disliked the thought of having the guns in the house, he knew they might be their only means of protection for the three women entrusted to their care.

* * * *

Amy could hardly believe anything that happened since she woke this morning. When the two men came to the door, she'd been terrified.

The memory of the angry voices at the telegraph office assaulted her mind. After what they did to her mother, would they hesitate for a moment to shoot Gary Tyler or anyone else in this house?

Even knowing Rex was a U.S. Marshal, didn't relieve her fears. She had no idea how he would be able to disarm two men with guns who also claimed to be U.S. Marshals.

This was her fault. She's brought this trouble to the Tyler farm. She was ready to tell the men at the door she was the person they wanted, but before she could get to her feet, Rex made his move.

The rest of what happened was a blur, leaving Amy in tears. Fear and relief mingled, bringing on sobs that wracked her body. With the men outside, Becky and Clara tried their best to comfort her, but with every nerve in her body on edge, she couldn't calm down.

"I've brought in Pa and Jesse's guns," she heard Eli say.

Bringing herself under control, she listened intently to the argument between Eli and his mother. She'd never wanted anything to do with guns, even though Phil insisted her mother keep a rifle in the telegraph office for protection.

As soon as the thought crossed her mind, she wondered why her mother didn't use the gun to protect herself. Did the men who beat her up catch her in a position unable to reach it? Wracking her brain she tried to remember seeing the gun when she returned to the office on Sunday morning. Even though she knew where it was kept and how to use it, she couldn't remember it being where her mother kept it. There was a distinct possibility the intruders took the gun when they left the office, making them doubly dangerous.

"Those men," she said, ending the verbal conflict between mother and son. "They aren't the same ones who beat my mother. Their voices were different, deeper."

"That confirms what they said outside," Clay said. "There are more than the two Rex arrested. You're right, Eli. We should bring in the guns. It's not that far to St. Louis from here. Amy and every one of us could be in danger."

"There's something else you should know. Ma kept a rifle in the office. I don't remember seeing it either time I was there. Should we be concerned about them coming to kill us?"

It was Clay who came to her side. "I doubt murder isn't anything we should be worried about. These men are interested in you, but they want you alive. As for the gun, I'm sure you weren't looking for it when you went back to the office. The men today were armed, but you're right, we should be prepared for future visitors. It's hard telling how many other men could be coming here looking for you."

* * * *

Clay fingered the pearl handle of the gun his mother once carried on a daily basis. It was still hard for him to believe the stories he'd read and heard since her death.

He remembered when his father wanted to teach him how to shoot. After two lessons, his mother found out what they were doing and forbid him ever to touch a gun again.

How strange it seemed to sit in his uncle's kitchen holding this gun. Eli loaded both weapons. Now Clay wondered if he'd be able to pull the trigger if more men from the mysterious St. Louis detective agency came to the farm.

The barking of the dogs again alerted Clay and Eli to someone in the farmyard. Clay's nerves kicked in as he tightened his grip on the pearl handle.

"It's Pa and Rex," Eli declared. "They're back."

Clay carefully loosened his grip and laid the now loaded revolver on the kitchen table.

"Did you boys have any trouble out here?" Gary said as he came into the house. He glanced down at the gun on the table. "Why are these in here?"

"Look, Pa if there are more of these guys looking for Amy, I thought it was best if we were armed," Eli explained.

"From what Rex found out while we were in town, you two hotheads are jumping to the wrong conclusions. The days of the old west are gone. These guns belong in the past and not in this house. Never in this house."

Clay watched as Eli unloaded the guns. He acted more like a chastised child than a grown man as he rewrapped them in the oilcloth. Clay had to admit he, like his uncle, would be happy to have the guns returned to their hiding place in the barn.

"From what I learned while I was in town, you shouldn't have worried about more intruders," Rex said. "Luckily the sheriff has a telephone, and I was able to talk to someone in my office. I waited while they contacted the detective agency. The men who were here on Saturday are in St. Louis. I authorized my office to arrest them in connection with Della's death. The people we spoke with in St. Louis couldn't or wouldn't say who hired them, but I'm sure it was

Montgomery Palter."

Clay watched as Amy nodded her agreement. "I've read a little of the beginning of Ma's journal. From what she wrote, he called her some vile names after my father died. He even implied I wasn't his granddaughter. If he didn't want me then, why does he want me now?"

The question Amy posed seemed to have no answer. Instead it brought on more questions. As much as Clay needed to learn of his ancestry, he now realized she had to come to grips with her past as well.

Chapter Ten

"If something had happened, would you have been able to pull the trigger on your ma's gun?" Eli addressed Clay as they walked to the barn to put away the guns.

"I doubt it," Clay replied. "Pa wanted to teach me how to shoot, but Ma was dead set against it. I was about twelve at the time, and it was exciting holding the gun and shooting at the target, which of course I missed by a mile. It was also terrifying. Until I first picked up Ma's gun, I'd forgotten how heavy they were. I'm just as happy not having to deal with something that lethal on a daily basis. How about you?"

"At least your pa taught you how to shoot a gun. I remember finding them when I was about fourteen and sneaking them out of the barn. I went out to the far field and shot it at an old dead tree. I don't think I fired off even three rounds when Pa showed up and gave me a lecture about the dangers of guns. Until today I've always known the guns were in the barn, but I hadn't touched them. I doubt I could have pulled the trigger, even if our lives were in danger."

Clay nodded, glancing at the oilskin his cousin carried. It was hard to think of anyone carrying a gun as easily as he carried his wallet. He knew his father wore a gun when he worked, but at home, he'd never seen a firearm in the house. Although knowing the truth about his mother's past, he understood her dislike for guns or anything connected with them. It was surprising to know she tolerated his father working as a U.S. Marshal.

"Living out west, did your pa do any hunting?" Eli said.

"He really didn't have the time. I know we ate wild game, but there were several hunters in the area we hired to bring us meat. It was Pa's concession to Ma's rule there could be no guns in the house."

"What about the gun your pa carried for his job?"

Clay laughed at the memory. "Pa always said he was the only marshal in his office who had to get his gun once he arrived at work. It was a private joke between the two of them. To my sister and me, he admitted he rather liked not having to bring his guns home. He told us he'd carried a gun for far too many years to have to bring it home now that he had a family."

Clay remembered his friends at school telling about their fathers taking them hunting. In one way, he envied them the experience but at the same time, he spent too many hours studying to be concerned with his lack of companionship with his father.

"What about your pa, does he hunt?"

"He does, but just in the fall. He doesn't use a gun though. He taught himself how to hunt with a bow and arrow. I have to admit, I enjoy hunting that way as well. It's more natural and makes a lot less noise. I'd like to go more often, but Pa says there's too much work to be done on the farm to hunt on a regular basis. I tend to agree with him. With everything that's been going on around here I'm getting way behind. The chores get done, but I've got horses to train, and I should be out cultivating the corn and cutting hay."

Having never lived on a farm, Clay had no idea what work the day-to-day operation of such a life entailed. He had to admit, he'd never done any real work in his life. The work he did with his father was far from the hard work Eli just described.

"Guess we have disrupted your lives. Is there something I can help you with?"

"Something tells me you have no idea what we do here. Of course, I wouldn't know what to do in college. Pa insisted I finish high school, but it wasn't my idea to study and go there every day. Pa said his one regret was that he didn't leave earlier for that fancy boarding school in St. Louis. He missed continuing his education by less than twelve hours when Caleb came and took him away."

"What do you mean?"

"That's right, the book didn't go into that part of the story. Caleb's desire was to have a gang made up of his sons. None of them went willingly, but Pa was the only one of the boys who didn't take to the life. From what Pa says, he couldn't pull the trigger, and the fact he never shot anyone was what saved his life at his trial. Thank God for people like Grandfather Otto. He saw something good in Pa and turned his life around."

"What do you mean turned his life around? If he never killed anyone, why would he need turning around?"

"Caleb didn't believe in God and neither did any of the boys. Your ma held onto her faith, but not Pa. It was Grandfather Otto along with Ma who brought him back to God."

"I know Ma was big on the whole 'God' thing, but going to school, I have my doubts. A lot of my friends there don't go to church and with the amount of studying needed to get good grades, I never seem to find the time to look for a church for myself."

Eli shook his head in disbelief. "I can't imagine not going to church on Sunday or reading the Bible at night. It's so much a part of my life I don't think I could continue on without it. Being a farmer, I know it's God who has a hand in everything we do. Just watching the horses foal, I know God is smiling at every new life."

Clay took what Eli said to heart. He knew his slip from faith would have disturbed his mother. Maybe the reason he came here was not to find out about his past, but to learn more about the God who ruled his future.

* * * *

Amy went up to the room where she'd been staying while at the farm. Reluctantly, she opened her mother's journal. Somewhere in these pages she hoped she'd find the truth. It wasn't that she didn't believe the letter her mother left for her, but there must be more to the rift between her mother and her paternal grandfather than it mentioned.

I was very lucky to find the job with Mrs. Palter, but I try to avoid her husband whenever possible. He is a gruff man and, although I know I'm a servant in his home, I don't like it when he treats me like an inferior.

James is home from college now, and he is so different from his father. He sought me out this morning when I was cleaning the upstairs bedrooms, and he kissed me. Then he told me he wants to court me. I didn't know what to say to his proposal. I can't believe he is interested in me.

Today I had to tell James that I'm going to have his child. I'm was so afraid he'd make me go away. Instead, we went down to the courthouse and got married. His father was livid when we came home to tell him our news. When Montgomery told us we could no longer live in the big house James said that suited him just fine, and we immediately moved to the guesthouse. James said it was part of his inheritance from his mother as well as the money she'd left in trust for him.

James is so excited to be a father to Amanda. He is so loving, he reminds me of my own father. Thank goodness she will never have to live hand-to-mouth the way my father and I did. James will always be there to provide for us.

"But he didn't live long enough to provide for us, did he, Ma? My grandfather must have been a horrible man for you to have changed our names and left St. Louis behind forever."

The journal held more entries, but would they give her the answers she so desperately wanted. She doubted it. There were always two sides to every story, but was she ready to get the information only Montgomery Palter could impart to her? If she were to go to St. Louis, would the man be truthful about why he wanted her in his life?

Unable to come to any concrete conclusions, she set aside the journal and lay down on the bed. Maybe a nap would chase away her fears and help her to make a decision where Montgomery Palter was concerned.

* * * *

Even though Clay offered his help with the farm work, both Eli and Gary turned him down. Instead he saddled one of the horses and rode into town with Rex.

"Will you be going back to St. Louis now that you've found out who broke into the telegraph office?" He spoke as they set the horses at an easy pace.

"I'm afraid so. I leave on the train tomorrow morning."

"I'd like to go with you."

Rex looked at him with a strange expression on his face. "Are you missing the big city?"

"Not really. I'd like to meet this Montgomery Palter. I worry about what might happen if he is able to get Amy to come to meet him. I guess I just want to test the waters. I'm sure my family will understand my motives."

"You're fond of her, aren't you?"

"I guess I am. I thought she was special when I first met her. I don't like the idea of this old man wanting her with him. The way it sounds, he's not one of the better people I'll ever meet."

Rex agreed and they rode the rest of the way in silence.

As soon as they approached the railhead, Clay saw Phil standing on the porch waving to him. "I got a wire for you Clay," he said once they dismounted and approached him. "I was just getting ready to drive out to the Tyler place to get it to you."

Clay took the yellow envelope and opened it. As he read the message, he began to smile. "Do you have a telephone?"

"I don't have one at the station, but I heard they have one over at the sheriff's office. I'm sure they'd let you use it. I take it that wire was good news."

Clay nodded and, along with Rex, made his way to the sheriff's office.

"Can I use your phone, Matt?" Clay said as they entered the office. "It will be long distance, but I'll get the charges and leave the money to pay for it."

Matt agreed and motioned toward the desk where the phone sat. Once Clay seated himself, Rex and Matt went into the back room of the office to give him some privacy.

He placed the call to his home and waited until Sally answered on the third ring. "Why Clay, I can't believe I'm talking to you halfway across the country. Are you all right?"

"I'm fine, Sally. Is Ellie there?"

"She sure is, and she's as excited as a little girl about this trip out to meet the rest of the family. She even wants me to come with her. Can you imagine that, Old Sally is going to go on a train and take a long trip?"

"That sounds lovely, Sally. Can I talk to my sister?"

Sally made a lengthy apology before handing the phone to Ellie.

"Hi, big brother," Ellie said, sounding more like her old self than she had since before the funeral.

"So, Sally got your butt out of bed and now you want to take a trip."

"She sure did. I decided I wanted to meet the rest of our family and get to know all the dirty little secrets our mother kept from us."

"I've learned a lot of them, Sis, and believe me there are a lot of things you don't want to know. When are you planning to come out?"

"Just as soon as you tell me it's all right with you."

"I have to go to St. Louis for a few days. When I get back, I'll get us a place to stay and then send for you."

"Why can't we stay at the farm?"

"There's a lot going on here that you don't know about. Uncle Gary and Aunt Clara have a lot on their plates right now. It would be best if we can find a place in town. I doubt you're be happy being stuck out in the country, and I'm sure Sally would be happier in a place of our own. I should be back by the middle of next week. I'll call you then."

He knew she was disappointed not to be able to hop the next train east, but after a lot of talking, he finally convinced not only Ellie but also Sally it would be best if they waited for a few days to make the trip to Loveland.

Chapter Eleven

"Rex is going to St. Louis tomorrow, and I'm planning to go with him," Clay announced at supper that night.

"Why?" Amy looked surprised.

"I want to check out this so-called grandfather of yours."

"Then I'm going with you."

"Oh dear. I don't know about this," Clara lamented. "It wouldn't look right for the two of you to be going to a big city like that alone. Don't you think you should be chaperoned?"

"Chaperoned." Gary nodded at his wife's word. "I think you have a good idea there. Eli can run things here and the two of us deserve a vacation. We could go along to keep the kids company and see the sights for ourselves. Maybe I might even look into buying us one of those automobiles Eli has been yammering about."

Gary's statement met with shocked silence around the table. "Are you saying we can modernize the farm?" Eli finally managed to say.

"I didn't say anything about jumping into anything that radical. We'll see how this automobile thing goes."

"It's not like riding a horse, Pa. How are you going to learn how to drive it?"

"If I'm not mistaken, Clay is more comfortable with an automobile than he is riding a horse. I'm certain he can teach me everything I need to know."

"Of course I can, Uncle Gary. It's a big investment, but Ma has had one for several years now. It made things easier for her than either riding a horse or driving a carriage. She enjoyed having her driver take her for long rides."

"Why would that be easier than driving a carriage?" Eli questioned. "I would think she'd like the freedom of driving herself and not having to depend on someone else."

Clay laughed at his cousin's statement. "The older Ma got, the more crippled she became. She needed help doing everything. I think having my sister and me took a toll on her. She also had a groom who took care of our horses and drove her wherever she wanted to go in the carriage. Of course, getting into the automobile was easier for her than getting into and out of the carriages we owned."

"You owned more than one carriage?" Clara said.

"Ma insisted on a closed carriage for winter and a surrey for summer. Pa also had his own sleigh for winter when riding his horse was impractical."

"I know you said your family was well off, but I never considered them having such vast wealth," Becky said.

"You have to remember most of the things we have were acquired over a long period of time. Added to that, Sally, my mother's maid, is like a member of our family. Oh, Sally. I almost forgot to tell you. Ellie and Sally are planning to come here when I get back from St. Louis. I inquired while I was in town and learned there's a house we can rent for the remainder of the summer."

"I'll hear nothing of that!" Clara exclaimed. "I won't have family renting a house in town when there's plenty of room here."

Clay laughed. "I think you have your hands full with the baby coming soon and Amy. I don't know if you'd be able to handle my sister, and I'm sure she wouldn't be happy so far away from town. Then there's Sally. She tends to be a bit bossy, and I doubt you'd want to share your kitchen with her. She certainly wouldn't be a guest. She's run our household ever since Ma and Pa got married, to say nothing of raising Ellie and me. Visiting will be nice, but I'm sure both of them will be more comfortable in town. I'm also going to look into buying an automobile when I get back. I noticed there is a garage on Main Street, and they have some vehicles for sale. I think I could strike a good deal on something used."

* * * *

With supper finished, Clay offered to clean up the kitchen while Becky helped Clara pack for the impromptu trip to St. Louis. He was pleased when Amy stayed to help him.

"I hope I didn't upset you when I offered to accompany you to St. Louis."

Clay looked up from the sink of hot sudsy water. "I was far from upset. I like the idea of going away for a few days with you. Of course, I hadn't expected Uncle Gary and Aunt Clara to come along with us."

"Clay Martin! Do you think I'd go away with you unchaperoned so that you could have your way with me?"

"Of course not. I planned on having two rooms. I also think it would be best if we had a united front when it comes to meeting with your grandfather."

"I'm not sure I want to meet him, but I don't want to run away again either. When we go into town tomorrow to get the train, I'm planning to ask Phil if I can have Mama's job when we return. I'm sure he'll be more than happy not to have to pay one of his employees to take messages. He knows I'm highly qualified. I should be. I've been working the telegraph key ever since I was old enough to write down the messages with accuracy."

Clay thought about the life Amy was prepared to embark upon. He didn't want to see her living in the solitude her mother imposed upon them for the past fifteen years. To be truthful, Clay wanted her in his life, but would she be able to accept the long hours his internship would involve?

Chapter Twelve

The next morning, Clay felt as though they were forming a parade as Gary drove the open carriage toward town with the three women and the bags they planned to take to St. Louis while Eli and Clay followed on their horses.

At the station, they met Rex. "You certainly have quite a group to see you off today."

"Amy wanted to go along to meet her grandfather. Since that would leave the two of us unchaperoned in St. Louis and Uncle Gary and Aunt Clara wouldn't have that, so they're going along with us to see the big city. Do you think we'll have trouble finding accommodations? We'll need three rooms."

"Two rooms," Gary interrupted. "There is no need to spend money on more rooms than that. Clara and Amy can share one room and you and I can share the other."

The thought of sharing a hotel room with his uncle wasn't exactly what Clay had in mind. In college, it was different. He and his roommate each had their own beds, but he wasn't thrilled about spending the night with another man in the same bed. By the look on Amy's face, he could tell she would be happier in a room by herself.

"This will be my treat," he finally said. "I doubt Amy would be any more comfortable sharing a room than I would. An extra room for the time we're in St. Louis wouldn't be that big an expenditure."

He could tell Gary didn't agree, but Clara was the one to end the discussion by agreeing with Clay.

Once they bought their tickets, he saw Amy take Phil aside. He knew she was inquiring about taking on the position her mother held for so many years. He ached at the thought of her being locked away in the telegraph office for the rest of her life. Since Della never had any help other than Amy it was entirely possible she wouldn't have any help either.

"It's all set. I will be able to work when I return from St. Louis. I did ask for more help since Mama and I did this together and Phil agreed with me. I think he's had more of manning the office this past couple of weeks than he can take. He realized it *does* take more than one person to do the job. Since I will no longer be hiding, I'll be able to have more time for myself than she ever did."

Clay wanted to applaud Amy for standing up for herself. If, in the end, she had to have a job to support herself, at least she would have help working in a position that wouldn't require all of her time.

Once they boarded the train, it was evident Clay and Rex were the only ones of the group who were accustomed to train travel. Everything excited Clara and Amy and, as far as Clay could tell, Gary was impressed as well.

The trip to St. Louis took four hours making Clay wonder why it took Montgomery Palter so long to locate his missing daughter-in-law and granddaughter. It was entirely possible he had no desire to find them before his health began to fail. What a shame Della and Amy lived in fear of a man who really didn't care.

Once they arrived in the big city, Clay felt immediately at home. He enjoyed the city of San Francisco and this Middle American city was as modern as the city he so loved. Automobiles mingled with horse drawn wagons and carriages. The streetlight weren't gaslights, but electric lights. Instead of a frontier town, St. Louis was a bustling city located on the banks of the Mississippi River that separated east from west."

"We never got into a city of this size," Gary said as the cab Clay hired took them the streets of the city to the hotel where Rex said they could find accommodations. "I heard about places like this, but Pa always hit small cattle towns. It was easier to rob the banks and get away from the law. Up until today, Loveland was the biggest town I ever saw."

"To be truthful, this is nothing compared to San Francisco. After the quake in '06, there was a great rebuilding. The people who live there are some of the most resilient people in the world. Of course, the shipping industry as well as mining has brought people from all over the world. It's a fascinating city with a multitude of cultures. I think you would enjoy it." From the look on Gary's face, Clay knew his uncle realized the comment was meant more for Amy's benefit than for anyone else.

The hotel was able to accommodate them, not with three rooms but with a room along with a two-bedroom suite. It was cheaper than the three rooms Clay originally planned to rent. He was more than willing to take the single room for himself and leave Amy to share the luxury of the suite with his aunt and uncle.

"This suite is beautiful," Clara declared. "I'm afraid this is too expensive for us. We couldn't possibly ..."

"Of course you can, Aunt Clara," Gary interrupted. "If I were to rent three single rooms, it would cost me a lot more than this suite and my single. I'm actually saving money and will be more comfortable having Amy share your suite rather than her having a room on her own. This is a big city, and you don't know who might be staying in a hotel of this size. I see it more for safety than anything else."

* * * *

The next morning they all met in the hotel dining room for breakfast. At that time, Gary and Clara made plans to see the sights of the city while Clay and Amy discussed hiring a car to drive out to the Palter mansion to confront Amy's grandfather.

"Do you want us to go with you?" Gary said.

"I don't think that will be necessary," Amy responded. "I need to do this alone. It will be enough to have Clay with me. I don't want to go in looking like we're an army coming to get him. I'm sure he knows what happened to the private detectives he sent to Loveland. Hopefully, he'll be expecting me."

By the time they finished eating, both couples agreed to meet back at the hotel for supper that evening and compare notes on the day's experiences.

Clay had no problems hiring a car and getting directions to the Palter mansion. It felt good once again to be behind the wheel of an automobile with Amy at his side. Staying on the Tyler farm had taken him back to his roots and made him miss the amenities of the modern day world.

Following the directions, Clay soon found himself driving on dirt roads away from the city. When he finally pulled into the drive leading to the mansion, he noticed the well-manicured grounds surrounding the veranda of the enormous home.

"May I tell Mr. Palter who is calling?" the man who answered the door asked.

Clay squeezed Amy's hand reassuringly. "You may tell him Miss Amy Baines and Mr. Clay Martin would like to have a few minutes of his time."

The man nodded. "I'll tell him. While you're waiting, you may have a seat in the library."

"We'd prefer to enjoy the delightful breeze on the veranda," Amy replied.

"Very well, Miss. I'll have refreshments brought out to you."

"Well, la-ti-da," Amy said once the man disappeared into the house. "We certainly didn't come all the way out here to have 'refreshments' on the veranda. What kind of a man screens his visitors?"

"A rich one who wants to know who's coming to see him. When I lived at home, Sally always answered the door and announced any and all visitors to my mother. I never knew why until my mother died. Once I heard the story of her life, I realized she was worried someone might want to find Laurel Morgan and bring back the ghosts of her past she wanted to keep buried."

Behind them a door opened and a maid in full uniform came out onto the veranda with a tray containing a pitcher of lemonade and three large glasses each containing a generous portion of the delicate yellow liquid and a slice of lemon. "Mr. Palter will be out to join you in a few moments. He said to make yourself comfortable and enjoy the lemonade."

Clay crossed over to where three white wicker chairs were arranged around a small round table where the maid placed the tray. "After you, Miss Baines," he said before following Amy so he could hold out the chair for her.

"I've never seen anything like this before. If I thought the suite was luxurious, it can't hold a candle to these comfortable chairs."

"I hoped you'd choose to sit on the veranda," a man said from behind them.

Clay turned to see an older man walking with an ebony cane with a gold handle and tip. Remembering his manners, he got to his feet to shake hands with the man he'd come to see.

"I'm pleased you agreed to meet with us, sir. I'm Clay Martin."

"I know who you are, young man. I learned all about you and your family when I found where my granddaughter was staying. I can tell you I don't approve of ..."

"Of what, Mr. Palter? Of my family's past or what we are today."

"Leopards don't change their spots. Once an outlaw, always an outlaw."

"I beg to differ," Amy said, getting to her feet. Even though she was tall for a woman she couldn't stand nose to nose with her grandfather. "That might be true in your case, but I've known the Tyler family for the past fifteen years and they are some of the best people I've ever had the privilege to meet. As for Clay, he knew nothing about his family until after his mother passed away this spring. I doubt any of them have robbed a bank or murdered anyone."

"Blood tells my dear. Just like blood tells with you. Your mother was a demanding woman, just like you. What do you want from me?"

"I think that's the question I should be asking you. You've sent two sets of men to Loveland to find me. The first men you sent beat my mother so badly it hastened her death. The second men came to the Tyler home with their guns drawn. I have no doubt they would have used them had it not been for the fact a real U.S. Marshal was there and put them under arrest. Now what do you want from me?"

Montgomery pulled out the third chair and motioned for Clay and Amy to take their seats. Once he took a long drink from his glass of lemonade, he turned toward Amy. "I always knew my son only married your mother because he believed she carried his child. Seeing you today, I have no doubts about the identity of your father. When he died, I felt as though I'd lost everything. My wife was gone and so was my only child. I wanted to blame your mother for his death, even though the doctors assured me he was sick and it was no one's fault."

"I've read my mother's journal and I know the nasty names you called her. I know she changed our names and moved out of St. Louis as soon as she could arrange it. A man with your means would have had no problem in tracing us to Loveland, so why did you decide to do this now?"

"I'm trying to come to grips with my past. You are my only living relative, and I wanted to meet you before I left you the bulk of my estate."

"Well, now you've met me. I doubt I'd be the one you'd want to leave everything to. I have no social graces. I've lived almost in seclusion all my life and am quite capable to taking care of myself. I don't think I'd fit into your social circle. All I want is for you to leave me alone to return to Loveland and the job that's waiting for me."

"Stop and think about what you're saying, Amanda," Montgomery pleaded. "I know what kind of life you face, and I can tell you the telegraph is as outdated as the stagecoach and horse and buggy. The train has replaced the stagecoach, just as the automobile will eventually replace the horse and buggy. Mark my words, the telephone is going to replace the telegraph within the next ten years. Once that happens, what will you do? Will you marry some dirt poor farmer?"

Clay watched as tears formed in Amy's eyes and ran down her cheeks. "I think you're being a bit harsh, Mr. Palter. How can you predict the future? How can you tell anyone who they might marry?"

The old man smiled for the first time since coming out onto the porch. "Well said, Mr. Martin, or should I say Dr. Martin. You see, I do my research well. I know you have one full year of hospital instruction left before you go into private practice. That is, if you return to San Francisco at the end of the summer. From what I've learned, you could easily return to Virginia City and never have to work a day in your life. Your parents left you very well off. Are those your plans?"

"If you know so much about me, then you know I'm dedicated to getting my degree and becoming a doctor. Where I chose to practice is something I won't know until I graduate and make my decision as to where to go."

"Good for you, my boy. Now, where you're concerned, Amanda, I do wish you would allow me the chance to get to know you. I'm dying and you won't be encumbered by me for long. Whether you want it or not, you are my heir and you will become a very wealthy young woman. I don't expect you to run my businesses, since I haven't been able to do the work for several years. Fortunately, I have excellent employees who love the companies as much as I do. They are loyal as well as honest and will protect your interests with their lives. Don't get me wrong, I have protected your money against anything that might happen with either the business or the economy in the coming years."

Amy took a deep breath and wiped at her tears before answering her grandfather. "With all of your wonderful research, I'm sure you know my mother legally changed our names fifteen years ago in an attempt to get away from you. I am not Amanda. I don't remember ever being called by that name. I'm Amy Baines. I live in Loveland, Missouri and I work for a living. What you're offering is tempting, but I have to think about it."

"Amy's right," Clay said, getting to his feet. "We came here to meet you and now that we have, I think it's time we leave to go back to the hotel. This whole ordeal has been hard on Amy. Because you wanted to find her, she lost her mother prematurely. Medically, she wasn't going to live much longer, but your private investigators robbed Amy of months or maybe a year she could have spent with her mother. I trust you already know where we're staying. Even though you aren't in the best of health, if you would like to discuss this further, you are more than welcome to meet us at the hotel dining room for dinner tomorrow at shall we say noon?"

The old man got to his feet and held out his hand to Clay. "Until tomorrow."

Turning to Amy he leaned in to kiss her cheek. It didn't surprise Clay when Amy turned away and made her way to the steps leading to the lawn from the veranda.

Chapter Thirteen

"How dare he? How dare that old man have you investigated? It's not like we're ..."

"Calm down, Amy. I don't blame him for wanting to know what kind of people are around you. For the rest of the day, let's forget about this visit. I saw a restaurant on the way here. I'll take you there for dinner. Tomorrow, we'll see if he's really interested in getting to know you. If he doesn't meet us at the hotel for dinner, you can write him off."

"What if he's right? What if the telephone does replace the telegraph? What will I do? How will I support myself?"

"I can tell you, I'd much rather use the telephone than to wait for a response from a wire. Just the other day I called my sister at home, and we talked as though we were standing right next to each other. This is the way of the future. I hope your grandfather was smart enough to invest in Mr. Bell's invention. As for how you're going to support yourself, what your grandfather is offering is a way for you to be independent and do anything you want with your life."

"You have enough to do whatever you want with your life. Why bother going to school?"

"Because going to school to become a doctor is what I want to do with my life. Without my parent's money, I probably wouldn't be able to afford it, either that or I'd have to have a job to support my studies. The way I see it, this is what your grandfather is offering you. I was intrigued when he said he has you protected against any economic problems. It would be interesting to find out how he plans to do it."

"But how can I accept any of it? I've lived my life in fear of this man. What would my mother think of me? How can I betray her?"

"You're not betraying her. She was a very frightened young woman when she left St. Louis. She'd lost her husband, was raising a little girl on her own, and was scared to death of her father-in-law. I'm not excusing that old man for the way he chose to mourn his wife and his son. He's a powerful man who's used to getting what he wants both in his professional and personal lives. As such, he's not entirely comfortable around people who don't think the same way as he does. When your mother and father married, he believed it was because they had a child on the way. Men like him don't understand love and how it can bridge all social barriers. I have no doubt your parents loved each other, but to his father, your mother was little more than an employee. Try not to be too harsh with him. In this day and age, there is no class distinction, but he was raised in an entirely different era."

Amy became quiet as Clay started the auto and drove away from the mansion and back to the restaurant he saw earlier as they drove out to meet with Montgomery. He knew she had a lot to digest and understand. He was sure the soft-spoken man they met this morning was not the man Della equated with her employer and also her father-in-law.

Like his mother always said, age tends to mellow people. He was certain she's been mellowed by age and the happenings in her life. He wondered if he would have liked the girl who rode with an outlaw gang and had the spunk to leave her abusive father and brother and become crippled for life for her efforts.

As a young boy, he asked his mother why she limped. She replied she was hurt in a riding accident when a young girl, but his father was able to look beyond the limp and still fall in love with her.

The memory hit him hard. There had been no riding accident. That is unless you could count being shot in the back and falling from your horse an accident.

He was so lost in his private thoughts, he almost drove past the restaurant where he planned to take Amy for dinner.

Why was his mother so secretive about her past? Did she think he'd love her any less?

He parked in front of the restaurant.

* * * *

84

"What did you find when you went out to meet with your grandfather?" Clara spoke after they finished placing their order for supper.

Amy sighed as she contemplated her answer. "He doesn't seem to be the monster I've always thought he was. H ... he wants to leave me his fortune. I told him I have to think about it, so he's meeting us here for dinner tomorrow at noon."

"Interesting," Gary said. "Why is it I have the feeling there's more to it than you're saying?"

"Because there is," Clay replied. "Once we got there, we found out he'd had not only me, but also you investigated. He knows more about our family than I do. Probably more than you do as well. He told me he knew I had one year left before I'd become a doctor. Considering I've only known of your existence for a little over a month, it's amazing he knew anything about me."

Amy contemplated what Clay said. At the time, she hadn't thought about how long she'd known Clay. In her mind, it felt as though they'd known each other forever, but considering her grandfather investigated him, she wondered how many other people in Loveland were researched once he knew where to find her.

"H ... he was so demeaning to Gary. I hope he doesn't show up tomorrow. It's hard telling what he'll say to you. I couldn't stand the thought of him saying those things to you?"

"What kind of things?" Gary urged.

"He said once an outlaw, always an outlaw."

Instead of being outraged, he laughed at her statement. "Is that all? Maybe Clay is lucky his mother never told him of her past. I've lived with people saying that all my life. Especially when I was selling them horses. Everyone thinks befcause I rode with Pa and Frank, I'm out to cheat them, steal from them, or murder them in their sleep. I've learned to ignore the words and show them with my actions that I'm not what they think I am."

Amy picked up on what Gary said. She didn't even know who she really was. She'd been Amy Baines for so long she didn't know how to be Amanda Palter. She wished she could talk to her mother and ask her what to do.

Sherry Derr-Wille

I am with you always, her mother's voice invaded her thoughts. The man you met today is not the one I ran away from fifteen years ago. I am with your father and we are both with you. God forgave me for not believing all those years. What your Grandfather is offering is sincere. Had your father lived, the money would have been his and eventually yours. Open your heart not only to your grandfather, but also to God.

Amy shook her head, unable to believe the words she'd just heard her mother say. Was she imagining things or were her parents really with her?

Believe what your mother has said, an unfamiliar male voice told her. I have always watched over both you and your mother. As a father, I couldn't be any more proud of you than I was today. It took a lot to stand up to my father, but believe me, he will be there to meet you tomorrow, and your future will be secure.

Chapter Fourteen

Clay met his uncle early the next morning, and together they went looking for automobiles Gary could buy.

"I still think it's a passing fad," Gary protested when they pulled up to the automobile dealership.

"Then why are you going through with this?"

"Eli wants us to come into the twentieth century. I suppose he's right. I remember being his age and wanting to modernize things around the farm. At that time, I said the same things to Clara's grandfather that my son is saying to me. When we get home, I'm going to look into getting electricity as well as a phone put in at the farm. The other day when Rex had to go into town to place a call to his office in St. Louis, I realized it would be something we could use at the farm in case of emergencies."

"Now you *do* sound like Ma. Pa and Jason pushed her into getting all those things a few years back. She dragged her feet, but once everything was installed, and she had an automobile to ride around in, she made everything sound like it was all her idea in the first place. Guess that's one of the things I loved the most about her. Until something was proved to be useful, she was reluctant to try anything new. By the time she got used to using it, she insisted anyone who was of importance should have the same things."

"Some things never change. Jesse was always the first to do things. Before we go in there, maybe I should tell you about the day she left Pa for good. We were just kids, but she was worried about having to prostitute herself for one of Pa's men. One day she told me she was leaving. Even knowing she probably had a price on her head, she had to get away from Pa and Frank."

"But Jason said she never had a price on her head," Clay interrupted.

"She didn't, but we were dumb enough to believe if we left we'd be swinging from a rope as soon as we hit the first town. Jesse didn't care, and, to be truthful, I didn't blame her. I knew what Pa really had in mind for her. It wasn't one of his men who were going to be using her as his whore. Pa made an arrangement to sell her to a whorehouse in Mexico as soon as we got back for the winter."

Clay thought he was going to be sick. How could a father, even one as evil as Caleb Tyler, sell his own flesh and blood into prostitution?

"I knew when she left, and I hoped she'd have a good life. Then one of Pa's men came back to camp and said he saw her riding toward town, but he took care of the problem and shot her in the back. I felt like I'd been the one who was shot. I doubled back and went looking for her. That's how I ended up meeting Russ and spending some time in the Loveland jail. That was the beginning of my new life as well as your mother's. I was lucky enough to have a man like Eli Otto on my side making my life much easier than the one your mother endured until Russ finally found her in Virginia City."

"Then the book was right. The reason she limped was because one of her father's men shot her in the back. I read it, I heard it, but until now I didn't want to believe it. I respect you and I loved my mother, but my grandfather isn't anyone who can stir any emotion rather than hatred in my heart."

"I can understand what you're saying. I felt that way for a long time before I turned everything over to the Lord. Are you at a point in your life where you can do that? I hope so."

Clay took a deep breath. If Gary asked him that four years ago, before he went off to college, he would have said an immediate yes. After being at school and not taking time for church, or even God, he knew he couldn't give his uncle the answer he was looking for.

"Right now, I doubt it. It's been a long time since I've been to church on a regular basis. I'm almost ashamed to admit that to you, because I know Ma would be disappointed in me. She put great stock in her belief. So did Pa."

Gary's smile was certainly not what Clay expected. "I already knew the answer to my question. As for your folks, that wasn't always the way things were. Russ lost his faith after Caleb and his men came to town and killed his first wife along with their unborn child. It was Jesse who brought him back, but after she shot Pa, she also lost her faith. Then it was Russ who brought her old Bible with him when he went to Virginia City looking for her. So don't worry, you aren't the first one in the family to struggle with a relationship with our Lord. Open your mind to Him and see what happens."

"Guess it wouldn't hurt. If I'm going to be a doctor, I won't be doing it on my own, I'll need some help. For some reason I decided I didn't need God if I had science. Maybe it's time to rethink my assumptions."

"Good," Gary said. "It won't happen overnight, so for now, why don't you help your old uncle pick out one of these new machines. On our way home, maybe you can teach me how to drive it."

As much as a Bible thumper as Clay first thought his uncle to be, he was seeing a different side of the man today. He wasn't asking Clay to come back to God immediately, just to think about it and see where life led him.

* * * *

Two hours later, Gary was the proud owner of a new Ford Model T touring car. It was agreed after the meeting with Montgomery Palter, Clay would return the car he'd hired and they would take a cab to pick up Gary's now acquisition.

By the time they returned to the hotel, Amy was a nervous wreck. "I was afraid you wouldn't get back in time. I don't know if I could have met with him alone," she lamented.

Clay took a liberty he'd refrained from before and took Amy in his arms. "You know I wouldn't leave you to face him alone. Uncle Gary is going to go up to his room and get Aunt Clara. Why don't we go into the dining room and get a table for five?"

He could feel her nod against his chest and allowed him to take her hand and lead her into the dining room. To his surprise, Montgomery Palter sat at a table set for six, along with another man Clay didn't recognize.

"Dr. Martin, it's good to see you as well as my granddaughter again. Won't you join us? I'm certain your aunt and uncle will be coming down for dinner soon, at least I anticipated seeing them today. That's why I requested a table for six."

Clay could feel Amy stiffen at the sight of her grandfather sitting at the table. "We were just coming in to make reservations for the five of us. I'm pleased to see you're already here and have taken that burden from us."

Clay held out a chair for Amy and watched as she seated herself. Before either of them could question the identity of the man with Montgomery, Gary and Clara joined them.

"Ah," Montgomery said, "you are very prompt, Mr. Tyler. Allow me to make the introductions. The gentleman who just joined us is Mr. Gary Tyler and his lovely wife, Clara. I've told you about them, as well as my granddaughter who prefers to be called Amy Baines although her real name is Amanda Palter and her friend, the soon to be good Dr. Clay Martin."

"You seem to be leaving someone out of these introductions," Clay said. "Who is the gentleman with you?"

"I'm Montgomery's lawyer, George Harrison. You must know Montgomery is a very wealthy man who will soon die, and he is looking for an heir to his estate. I know the story of how you and your mother disappeared without a trace and believe me I can understand your mother felt you both had to leave St. Louis in the way she did. I remember the time well, and I told Montgomery he would regret his actions, but he was bitter over the loss of his wife to say nothing of his son."

"I'm a medical student, and I don't know much about the law. What I do know is the way you treated your daughter-in-law and granddaughter doesn't sound like a loving grandparent to me. Yesterday you questioned my grandfather and since then I've learned he wanted to sell my mother into prostitution. How much different is that from shunning your son's widow and daughter because you're grieving? Didn't you, for one minute, think they were grieving, too?" For the first time, Clay saw Montgomery's smug façade begin to crack.

"To me, Darlene was the maid my wife hired. After my wife's

90

death, I paid little attention to the hired help, but apparently my son felt differently. When he told me he was in love with her, I encouraged him to look for someone in our own class. That's when he said she was going to have a baby and with or without my blessing, they were going to be married. What could I say? I couldn't stop him, but I didn't have to bless their union. I did allow them to live in the guesthouse at the back of the property."

"How generous of you," Amy interrupted.

"I'm not proud of the way I treated your parents, but that's just the beginning of the story. I noticed the doctor's buggy at their door, but I thought it was for the baby. Later, I learned about James' illness. Within a week, Darlene came to my door and told me of his death. I was devastated. James was the last member of our family and here was this little maid asking me to support her and the child. I told her to get away from me, but then she begged me to give her a job as a maid and allow her to stay in the guesthouse with the baby. Unfortunately, I told her I knew how she tricked my son into marrying her so she could have a name for her bastard."

Amy gasped and began to sob. "If I'm my mother's bastard, why are you trying to leave me your fortune? Why would you send someone to Loveland to beat up my mother and threaten the people who were kind enough to take me into their home?"

"Perhaps I can explain that," Mr. Harrison interjected. "Just recently, while cleaning out the guesthouse, Mr. Palter found his son's journal. It was then that he learned the truth about how much your father loved not only your mother, but also you. As much as it bothered Mr. Palter, he continued reading all the entries including the details of their love affair. As for the men who came to Loveland not once but twice, he had no idea they were anything but reputable private detectives. It was his intention to get information about your whereabouts, not to do it violently. What Mr. Palter is offering you is a wonderful opportunity. He's not looking for your love, but he wants to know you will be able to lead a comfortable life without any financial worries."

"I've been thinking about this ever since our meeting yesterday morning," Amy said. "Before my mother died, I was under the impression my grandfather was Adam Baines and he was someone who hated me. When I learned your real identity, I was angry. How could someone with your wealth allow my mother to work herself to death in order to support us? After meeting you yesterday, I've had some long talks with Clara Tyler. She told me about second chances. If Eli Otto could take a man accused of robbery and murder into his home and help him to become a productive citizen of Loveland, perhaps a leopard can change his spots. Aren't those the words you said to us yesterday, Grandfather?"

Montgomery reached across the table to take Amy's hand. "Thank you, Amanda, I mean Amy. I don't have much time left, but I would like to get to know you. If you are going to inherit my fortune, I'd like to give you a taste of the life you should have been living if it hadn't been for my misguided treatment of both you and your mother."

Chapter Fifteen

It broke Clay's heart when he learned Amy decided to stay in St. Louis and take Montgomery up on his offer.

"I don't understand why you would stay here with him," he pleaded as she packed her few belongings in her traveling bag.

"Over the past few days, I've heard stories about not only my family, but also about yours. What would have happened to your uncle as well as your mother, if someone hadn't given them a second chance? You and your sister might not have been born and Eli and Becky wouldn't be giving Gary and Clara another grandchild. My mother and I had a hard life, but it was a good life. Now that she's gone, I need to get to know my family."

"Get to know him and ..."

"The money will be something to give me a comfortable life, but it's not the main reason I want to get to know my grandfather. Maybe I can give him some peace before his time on this earth is ended. I didn't have a chance to do that for my mother, since I didn't know she was sick. As for my father, I was too young to know what was going on in his life. Hopefully, I can bring some comfort to an old man and learn of my heritage in the process. Please, Clay, try to understand what I'm saying."

Clay took her in his arms and for the first time he kissed her lovingly. "Whatever you do is what you have to do. I completely understand. Just remember, I'm going to be staying in Loveland until the end of the summer. After that, here is where you can reach me." He handed her a piece of paper with the address of the dorm where he would be staying for the last year before he became a doctor and opened his own practice wherever he would be needed. "If you ever need me for anything, you can always call on me."

"Oh Clay, you know I will. I understand we hardly know each other, but I think I'm in love with you. When Grandfather is gone, I hope you will want to get better acquainted and maybe ..."

Clay kissed her again, "There is no maybe. I feel the same way and will be looking forward to whatever the future holds for us. For now I need to get back to Loveland and deal with my sister and Sally."

"I hope to meet them someday. I'm sure I'd like Ellie. As for Sally, she sounds like a wonderful person."

Clay helped her carry her bag down to the lobby where she was met by Montgomery Palter along with his driver.

"How much longer will you and the Tyler's be staying in St. Louis?" Montgomery asked.

"We're leaving tomorrow morning. I'll be meeting my sister in Loveland and plan to spend the summer there getting to know our family better."

"If you decide to come back to St. Louis before you leave for San Francisco, please feel free to come and stay at the mansion. There is no reason to spend money on a hotel when I have more bedrooms than I can ever begin to fill."

Clay reluctantly shook hands with Montgomery and gave Amy a chaste peck on the cheek. As much as he wanted to take her to the nearest justice of the peace and make her is wife, he refrained. He'd decided to take this summer to get to know his family, and he certainly couldn't deny Amy the same privilege.

* * * *

"You didn't want to leave her there, did you, Clay?" Gary observed as they drove away from the hotel and headed toward Loveland.

"I'm torn. I can't offer her anything to compare with what Montgomery Palter is prepared to give her. I don't fault her for wanting to get to know her grandfather and accept what he has to offer her."

"If the two of you love each other, God will find a way to get you together," Clara said. "I remember when I loved Gary and knew I could never have him because he didn't believe the same way I did. God touched his heart and the rest as they say is history."

Clay contemplated what his aunt said and combined it with Gary's suggestion he open his mind to the Lord. He didn't know if the Lord would touch him the way He touched other members of his family.

They pulled out of St. Louis and made their way to Loveland. It was a four-hour trip on the train that stopped in numerous small towns. By driving they made it in a little over three hours. As soon as they pulled into town they stopped at the train station to let them know of Amy's decision to remain in St. Louis for as long as necessary, considering her grandfather's condition.

"Amy sent us a wire yesterday telling us of her decision," Phil said. "I'm already looking for a new telegraph operator. I also have a wire for you. It's a good thing you got in today."

Clay looked at him skeptically as he took the yellow envelope containing the wire that came for him.

ARRIVING   ON   FRIDAY   MORNING   TRAIN
*   –SALLY*
AND I DIDN'T WANT TO STAY AWAY ANY LONGER—SEE
YOU WHEN WE ARRIVE
*   –ELLIE*

"Friday," Clay said looking up. "That's tomorrow. When did this arrive?"

"Right after you left on Sunday. Are you ready for her arrival?"

Clay shook his head. "I looked at a house to rent, but I didn't tell them to save it for me. I don't even have an automobile to pick them up tomorrow. It looks as though I have a lot of work to do."

"I thought as much. I know it's against the rules, but since I didn't know when you were planning to get back, I contacted Eli. Between him and Becky, they've been taking care of the details here in town. The only thing they didn't do was look into an auto for you. I made some inquiries around town and found someone who is willing to let you use his vehicle for the remainder of the summer. His name is Ed Parks, and he's been very sick lately. He probably won't be able to drive for the remainder of the summer, and his wife won't touch the thing. He's glad you'd be driving and taking care of it."

Clay breathed a sigh of relief. He was glad he'd told the family about his plans so Eli could take care of the arrangements before Ellie's train arrived in the morning.

Clay returned to where Gary and Clara waited for him in the automobile. "Prepare yourselves, Ellie and Sally are arriving on tomorrow morning's train. I'm thankful to Phil for breaking security and telling Eli of the wire. He's taken over the preparations, and Phil has arranged for me to hire an auto for the rest of the summer. At least the house I was looking to rent is furnished, so that burden was taken from Eli."

"I do wish you would allow Ellie and Sally to stay at the farm. With Amy deciding to remain in St. Louis, we have plenty of room."

"Believe me, Aunt Clara, Eli and Sally will be much happier in town. Besides you already have two women in your kitchen. You certainly don't want to add Sally to the mix. She's a very controlling woman. Don't get me wrong, I love Sally with all my heart, but she also takes some getting used to. It will be better this way. If I know Sally, she's already planning a dinner party for the family. It's something she enjoys doing. Mother always loved Sally's parties, because she could associate with the best people in Virginia City without having to lift a finger. I'm afraid Ellie is much the same way. In other words, Sally has spoiled the two of them rotten."

Chapter Sixteen

Clay and Eli waited at the station on Friday morning for the train from the west to arrive. It wasn't hard to spot Sally as she stepped onto the platform followed closely by Ellie. Looking at his sister's fashionable clothes he wondered how she would fit into this rural setting.

"There's my lamb," Sally declared as she waddled across the platform to where Gary stood with Eli. "I was afraid you'd be wasted away to nothing. Praise the Lord you're eating well."

To Clay's embarrassment, Sally hugged him as though he'd been gone from her watchful eye for years rather than weeks. It was the same greeting he received every time he returned home from school over the past four years.

Ellie didn't hold back either as she rushed to where Clay and Eli were standing and threw herself into her brother's arms. "I just couldn't stay in Virginia City a moment longer. You're out here meeting our family and having all sorts of adventures, and I've been stuck at home. I just hate being left out of things."

"As I recall, dear Sister, you took to your bed after the funerals. When I left, you vowed you were going to die just to be with Ma and Pa."

"That was then, this is now. Sally showed me just how silly I was being. She told me everything she knew about Ma and Pa and insisted I read that damnable book. What a bunch of garbage. That certainly couldn't have been our mother. Maybe Uncle Gary was as bad as the book made out. Does he wear a six gun and rob banks and such?"

From behind them, Clay heard Eli's hearty laughter. "You've got a lot to learn, Ellie. I'm your cousin Eli and I'm under strict instructions to bring the two of you out to the farm for dinner. Clay has rented a house for the three of you, but Ma insists you belong with us. I tend to agree with Clay, but you must know how hard it is to go against your mother."

Sally wiggled her way through until she stood in front of Eli. "Pay no mind to this child. I've been trying to tell her Loveland, Missouri is no longer part of the wide west and you don't have shootouts in the streets the way them dime novels tell it. It's no wonder Miss Laurel-I mean Miss Jesse never wanted these young'uns reading them. I'd be pleased to go out to your farm and meet your mama, but not until we stop at the house Clay has for us. I want to clean up and at least put our bags away."

Clay winked broadly at Eli. "I told you Sally is something else. We'd planned on stopping at the house and showing you around town before heading out to the farm."

After picking up the traveling bags, Clay made arrangements for the trunks to be delivered before helping Sally and Ellie into his rented auto.

"This is almost as nice as the auto we have at home," Ellie observed. "I honestly expected a horse and buggy. Guess I have a lot to learn about living in the country."

"I guess you do," Eli said, as he slid into the back seat with her, leaving the front seat open for Sally. "When I picked up Clay at this very station, I did so with a horse and wagon. I could tell by the look on his face, he was certain he'd arrived in the middle of nowhere."

"Then this isn't your auto?" Ellie asked in her flirtiest voice.

"Hardly. Pa just bought one when he went to St. Louis with Clay. I'm pushing him to have electricity, indoor plumbing, and a telephone installed at the farm. I'm afraid you're going to find we're pretty much stuck in the nineteenth century."

Ellie's tinkling laughter made Clay smile. She was going to be in for a surprise when she met Becky. Even if Eli was her first cousin she wasn't above flirting. It could turn out to be an interesting summer.

"Sunday's coming up," Sally said turning in her seat to face Eli. "Does you all go to church?"

"We most certainly do. I'm sure you and Ellie will be a welcome addition to our congregation. Maybe we'll even be able to persuade Clay to join us on Sunday mornings."

From the corner of his eye, Clay saw a smile cross Sally's face. "I'm sure his mama knew he didn't go to church on a regular basis when he was at school, but she never wanted to admit it. Bless that poor child's heart, she didn't want to think the worst of anyone. She was so content in her faith, after Mr. Russ came to find her that is, she thought everyone else in her life felt the same way. I tried to tell her what was going on in her family, but she wouldn't listen to me. Maybe it was better that way. She was always a delicate flower."

Delicate flower? What a perfect way to describe his mother. She was the ultimate delicate flower. Maybe that's why he'd had such a difficult time in accepting the Jesse Tyler Gary knew and loved.

* * * *

Clay held open the door to the house he'd rented for them for the summer. He hoped his choice would be acceptable for his sister and Sally.

"Oh, Clay, this is just perfect," Ellie gushed. "I'm so glad Sally and I decided to come for the rest of the summer. It's much cozier than our house in Virginia City. It will be just like playing house, won't it, Sally?"

Clay watched Sally's reaction to what Ellie said. From the faraway look in her eyes, he knew she was already missing Sam. They'd been married for well over thirty years, and, if he wasn't mistaken, this was one of the first times the two of them had been separated.

"Of course it will, Baby. You know I'll be missin' my Sam, but he has to stay in Virginia City to keep an eye on Mr. Jason. He ain't a young man, you know, and he misses Miss Laurel something fierce. If he lasts the year it will be only by God's grace. I didn't want to tell you like this, but it's best if you're prepared."

"What Sally is trying to say is that once something happens to Jason, you and I will be the owners of The Mother Lode," Ellie explained. "Just before we left to come here, he told me he'd planned to leave everything to Mother and Father. He wanted to let us know he was changing his will, so we could be prepared for the future."

Clay could feel the tears he'd shed for his mother threaten to spill from his eyes at the thought of losing Jason. The man had been a surrogate grandfather for his entire life. Even though The Mother Lode was a gambling house with ladies who once lived upstairs, Jason was never anything but a loving friend to the family.

He continued to contemplate what Sally said, while she and Ellie changed from their traveling clothes to something more suitable to wear to the farm. Knowing he would be leaving for school as soon as he returned, Clay knew he would want to leave Loveland a little earlier than planned so he could get to see Jason for what might be the last time.

"We're ready to go," Ellie said, breaking into Clay's thoughts. "We have been for the past ten minutes, but you were off someplace in your mind."

"I guess I was thinking about Jason. Is he really sick?"

"Not sick, just broken hearted. Mother was very special to him. I've tried to tell him he'll always be part of the family. He told me he knew that, but he would never stop missing her."

* * * *

Clay knew he would miss staying at the farm. He'd come to love the chores he'd helped Eli do to say nothing of the beautiful Clydesdale horses his uncle raised.

"This is what we call home," Eli said, as he helped the two women out of the auto. "I know it's not what you're accustomed to, but we love it."

Sally got out of the car and stretched. "Compared to where I grew up, this place is paradise. What a beautiful home. I'm looking forward to meeting your parents."

As though on cue, Gary and Clara stepped out onto the porch followed closely by Becky. Clay took Ellie's hand and led her toward the family she'd come all this way to meet.

"Uncle Gary, Aunt Clara, this is my sister Ellie."

For the first time since her arrival, Clay saw his sister on the verge of tears.

"I wish we'd known about you before this. There is so much about our mother's life we didn't know until after she died. I've been reading her journals and I know how much she loved you. Unfortunately, I also learned she couldn't come to grips with the life she lived as a child."

Ellie's comment caught Clay completely off guard. While he'd been in Loveland meeting the family and learning all its dirty little secrets, Ellie had been reading the journals, he couldn't bring himself to read. If he had, would any of this come as such a surprise? He doubted it.

"Come along, Clay," Ellie urged. "I can smell something delicious cooking from out here. It would be a shame if it were to get cold."

Clay agreed. His Aunt Clara could prepare a meal that was the rival to anything their cook ever served or anything he'd ever eaten at The Mother Lode. Suddenly, he was hungry and ready to partake of the dinner waiting for them in the house.

* * * *

With dinner over, the women worked at cleaning up the kitchen, and Clay went out onto the porch with Gary and Eli to enjoy a smoke. Feeling more comfortable around this table than he had been before, Clay accepted one of Eli's cigarettes while Gary casually lit his pipe.

"I'm going to miss being here," he confessed.

"You don't have to leave, you know," Gary said. "Being summer, we could use another pair of hands and you know Ellie and Sally are more than welcome to stay here. I'm sure you could get back the rent you paid for the house in town."

"I'd like to take you up on your offer, but I've said it before, you don't want to have two extra women trying to run your kitchen. Besides, if Ellie were to stay you'd have to put in indoor plumbing, electricity, and a telephone. I'm the first to admit, my sister is spoiled. I guess I am too, for that matter. The difference is I've been on my own for the past four years and know how it is to be away from all the comforts of home."

"Then you agree with Eli about modernizing this place?"

Clay thought for a moment. He didn't want to insult his uncle, but he did miss indoor plumbing and electricity. "It's the coming thing," he finally commented.

"You're diplomatic, but I'm beginning to agree with you. When we were in St. Louis, I enjoyed not having to go outside to use the outhouse, and I have to admit the electricity was nice. I'm sure Eli and Becky will be pleased to know I plan to modernize the farm. I was hoping you'd be able to stay with us and help with the construction."

"Uncle Gary is right," Ellie said. "The house in town is cozy, but I came here to get to know my family. I didn't come to sit in town while the people I want to know are here. Aunt Clara and I were talking while we cleaned up the kitchen. Even Sally agreed we're needed out here. With summer coming on there will be garden produce to be canned, and she is looking forward to helping with that. Until the baby is born, I can use the fourth bedroom upstairs and since there are two single beds Sally can stay with me. I know you thought you were doing us a favor, but this is where I'd rather be."

Clay was surprised by Ellie's reaction. Seeing her in her fashionable bob haircut and mid-calf length skirt made him wonder how she would adapt to the simple life the farm offered.

He thought of the life they'd lived in Virginia City. His mother was treated like the queen of the city, and Ellie usually reaped the benefits of such a life. There was never a time he could remember her wearing anything other than the latest fashion. His mother often sent to New York as well as San Francisco for the best dresses for her daughter. They'd also enjoyed the enormous wall of books that filled three of the four walls of the room they called the library. They both had a love of reading, but he doubted Ellie ever did a day of work in her life.

"Are you sure about this?" Clay finally spoke.

"Of course she's sure," Clara replied. "I told you when you first said Ellie and Sally wanted to come here to visit, that I won't tolerate family being in town and not staying at this house. By the time the garden is ready for harvesting, Becky will be almost ready to deliver her baby. To be truthful, she'll be so uncomfortable in the heat she won't be much help. When I mentioned the garden, Sally said she'd love taking over as well as tending it, but also to do the canning. She's already talking about how she wants to do some sewing for not only this baby, but also for the one Laura will be having."

It didn't take long for Eli to suggest they make a trip back to town to pick up the luggage and advise the owners of the house the plans had been changed. His cousin seemed so eager, Clay wondered if this had been the plan from the very beginning.

"What about the rent I paid?" Clay said once they pulled his rented automobile out onto the dirt road.

"Well, Becky and Ma think alike and so I told the owner I would tell you the house was rented and he'd hold it for you, but I didn't actually say you'd pay anything. I was sure once Ellie and Sally got here Ma would be able to talk them into staying with us. You'll see, everything will work out just fine."

Chapter Seventeen

Within a week, having the whole family working together on the farm seemed as natural as living in the mansion in Virginia City to Clay. While Gary and Eli worked in the field, Clay and Ellie orchestrated the remodel of the house. The power company ran an electrical line to the farm, and the phone company installed the new phone, even though Clara kept saying she wanted no part of it.

This morning, a builder from town was coming out to remodel the downstairs bedroom to accommodate the new bathroom, including the latest model of claw foot tub. Eli also found someone in town who could bring running water into the house. Gary decided to install a water heater to make things easier for both Clara and Becky.

Any worries Clay harbored about Sally fitting into the Tyler household were squelched the first day they were there. Rather than trying to take over Clara's kitchen, Sally was more than happy to tend the garden and sit in the sun on the porch to work on her sewing.

"It's time for me to rest and do something I really enjoy," she'd told him. "I've been your mama's maid for more years than I care to remember. I've loved every minute of it, but now I'm ready to do things like gardening and sewing. You of all people know the gardens I planted in Virginia City never amounted to a hill of beans. Here things grow because the good Lord sends the right amount of sunshine and rain, to say nothing of providing the proper soil."

At least once a day, Clay found an excuse to go into town and check at the telegraph office for word from Amy. Today would be no different from any of the other days he'd made the trip to town. He was ready for the new telegraph operator to tell him there were no messages for him from St. Louis.

"Clay, it's good to see you," Phil said before Clay could go into the office. "I know you've been waiting for a message from Amy. If I didn't see you soon, I was going to send a boy out to the farm to deliver this wire, along with the one I received for you this morning from Virginia City."

Clay's heart stopped beating for a moment. The excitement of hearing from Amy was overshadowed by the possibility of bad news from home. If something happened to Jason while both he and Ellie were out of town how could he possibly forgive himself?

As much as he wanted to read the wire from Amy, he opened the one from Virginia City first.

> *HAVE NO PHONE CONTACT FOR YOU – JUST WONDERING HOW ELLIE AND SALLY ARE DOING IN LOVELAND – IF YOU CAN USE A PHONE, YOU KNOW THE NUMBER AT THE MOTHER LODE*
>
> *-JASON*

Clay wiped a tear from his eye. In his quest to reach Amy, he'd completely forgotten contacting Jason. The poor man must be worried sick. With the relief of knowing there was nothing wrong at home, he opened the wire from Amy.

> *GRANDFATHER HAS TAKEN A TURN FOR THE WORST— HAVE RECEIVED YOUR WIRES—WILL CONTACT YOU WHEN IT IS FINISHED*
>
> *– AMY*

He ached for Amy. It wasn't that long ago when she lost her mother, and now she was seeing the grandfather she never knew and always feared though the last days of his life.

* * * *

"What would you like for me to read to you today?" Amy said, as she entered Montgomery's bedroom.

105

"You ask me that question every day. We've worked our way through more than one of the classics. What I would like to hear today is the word of my Lord from the Bible."

Amy's hands trembled as she touched the book her grandfather held Holy. Her mother's words saying she refused to go to church because it was something her father-in-law loved, and if that's what a Christian was she wanted no part of it.

"Are you sure you want me to read this? I've never read anything out of this book. I ... I don't believe."

"I know you don't, and I understand the reason you have no faith. That doesn't mean our Lord doesn't care about you. He loves all his children and, believe me, you are a child of God."

"How can you say that when I've never even been to church?"

"Your mother was justified in what she did. As her child, you stood by her, and I'm sorry she was taken from you before her time. If I had anything to do with it, I ask you for your forgiveness. I've already asked God to forgive me, and he sent me you. My favorite reading is the Twenty-Third Psalm, but I think the one you should read, not for me, but for you is John 3:16. Hopefully, it will give meaning to the faith you were born into."

"I don't understand what you're saying."

"When you were born, your mother and father both insisted you be baptized. I have relived that day ever since you and your mother disappeared from my life. It took me a long time to understand the role I played in your disappearance. By the time I did, it was even harder for me to find where you'd been hiding all these years. I'm not asking you to jump into anything, but please read the words of our Lord and open your heart."

Amy opened the well-worn book and read the words of the Twenty Third Psalm and finished reading the verse from John her grandfather wanted to hear. As she said the last word, she noticed he'd fallen asleep. Rather than leave the bedroom, she began to read more of the Bible.

As she read the words, she realized her mother had quoted the same passages many times throughout her life. It was evident that at one time her mother not only read but memorized the passages she was now reading.

I haven't gone to church but I have given you these words to live by. Maybe it's time you read them for yourself. You've found your grandfather and learned he's repented of his sins. With my death, I began my new life with my heavenly father as well as the man I loved all my life. God never gave up on me. Open your heart and let Him get to know you.

Amy awoke with a start. The dream about her mother was so vivid it seemed as though she would find her standing at her bedside. Never before had her dreams been as real nor the words as moving as the ones she'd just encountered. Every word her mother spoke resonated in her memory.

"That must have been some dream," her grandfather said once she was fully awake.

"It was. I was reading the Bible and must have fallen asleep. I dreamed of my mother, and she said the same thing you did. She said I should open my heart to God. Can it be possible that I am a child of God? Do you think He will accept me?"

"Oh, my dear child, I know He will accept you. It's not even a question. The question is if you will accept Him?"

* * * *

Clay stared at the wire he held in his hand. It didn't seem possible he'd left Amy in St. Louis to get to know her grandfather. At the time, he'd heard about how sick Montgomery Palter was, but he didn't believe it for a minute. He was certain it was a ploy to get Amy to stay with him. Now he knew everything he'd been told was true.

Amy's wire said her grandfather had passed quietly in his sleep, and she would be remaining in St. Louis until the estate was settled. She now knew what she wanted to do with her future.

"If this woman is the one you were meant to be with, the Lord will bring her back to you," Sally said once he informed the family of what was happening in Amy's life. "God has a way of bringing the right people into our lives. Your pa waited a long time to find your ma, but God wanted them to be together, and, when the time was right, he came to Virginia City to claim the woman he loved. It was then that the job with the U.S. Marshal's office opened and allowed them to stay where she felt safe and loved."

Clay thought of his parents. Was it God who brought them together or was it fate? As far as the job at the Marshal's office, he always thought Jason had a hand in it.

* * * *

Throughout the summer, Clay worked on various projects for the ongoing modernization of the house and barn. Although Gary objected, Clay was certain he enjoyed not only the running water and the indoor bathroom, to say nothing of the brighter light produced by the electric lights.

"I have always like to read at night. I have to admit this makes it much easier."

Clay smiled to himself, remembering how his parents fought the same things until they were installed in their home.

As he had earlier in the summer, Ellie begged for information on the family neither of them ever knew. Her reaction came as a surprise. Even reading the headstones at the cemetery didn't bring her to the tears and depression he'd experienced at the same sight.

"I'm surprised at how well you're taking this," he said on the day they left the cemetery.

"Sally told me a lot more of the story than Jason told the two of us before you left Virginia City. She even insisted I read Ma's journals. I was better equipped to come here than you were. It doesn't matter, not really. The two of us are a product of our parents and not of their pasts."

Clay vowed to read the journals but knew it wouldn't happen until he finished his last year of schooling to become a doctor. If he thought the last four were hard, this one would be extremely difficult. Working at the hospital for up to sixteen hours a day would be draining. There would be no room for finding the past.

Whatever he found on this trip would have to suffice until he was able to establish himself in private practice somewhere in the country. He'd always seen himself working in a big city like San Francisco, but after this summer, he saw the need in rural communities like Loveland. In his mind, at least at the present time, was where he saw his future. The lure of big money in the city was now overshadowed by the need to practice medicine for people who really appreciated the doctor taking care of their needs.

Chapter Eighteen

By the middle of August, Clay was ready to leave for San Francisco to start his last year of medical school. At the same time, Clara prepared for her trip to Peoria to be with Laura for the birth of their first grandchild.

"Don't you worry about a thing here," Sally informed her. "Miss Ellie and I plan to stay for as long as necessary. It takes a lot of work to keep this family going, and Becky needs her rest more than ever. I may not be the cook you are, but I can keep this family fed. Your place is with your daughter and new grandchild."

"What about Sam?" Clay said.

"Sam and I talk on the telephone once a week. He knows I need to be here. Of course, you will be seeing him when you stop in Virginia City on your way to San Francisco."

Clay took a minute for what Sally said to sink in. In his mind, he wanted to stop in Virginia City and spend time with Jason, but hadn't made any concrete decision. To have Sally suggest something he only considered, he knew it would be the right thing to do. It wouldn't be hard to for him to spend a few days in his childhood home. In fact, he was certain it would do him good.

* * * *

The train pulled into the Virginia City station, and Clay wondered who would be meeting him this early in the morning. The sun was barely up. Even if no one met him, he could take his traveling bag and walk the short distance to The Mother Lode.

As soon as he stepped from the train, he recognized Jason and Sam waiting for him. Seeing them, reminded him of how much he missed living in Virginia City and seeing Jason and Sam on a daily basis.

"It's been a long summer without you, Ellie, and Sally here," Jason greeted him. "How are they doing?"

Clay smiled and followed Jason to where Sam had parked the automobile. "It's been a summer of discovery. I even held the gun my mother used to carry on a daily basis. Of course I met Uncle Gary and Aunt Clara as well as my cousin Eli."

"I think you met someone else. What about the young woman Sally says you left behind?"

"Amy is finding herself and when she's finished, I'm sure she will have found a man more to her liking than me in St. Louis. Like Sally says, if it's meant to be, it will happen. For now I have to concentrate on getting my degree. Ellie says we're the product of our parents, but not their pasts. At this point I'm happy my last name is Martin and not Tyler. Of course, that didn't save me when Amy's grandfather had me investigated."

"I had an investigator visit me here shortly after you left to go to Missouri. I figured something was up, but I could see no reason not to tell them the truth. Your mother tried to hide from the past and it still found her. It took a lot of persuading to get her to accept who and what she was. She finally came to grips with her identity, but I doubt she ever completely accepted it. If she had, she wouldn't have kept everything a secret from you and Ellie. I'm sorry you had to learn of it in this way, but she wouldn't allow either me or your father to tell you the truth. Maybe its best you spent this summer on a quest to find your heritage."

* * * *

The mansion looked no different from when he left over three months ago. Unfortunately, the feeling was different. He couldn't hear his mother's laughter or smell her perfume. With Ellie gone, her constant chatter was silenced.

"Mr. Clay, it's good to have you home," their cook, Constance, greeted him when he walked into the kitchen.

"I won't be here long. I honestly didn't expect to find anyone here. Who have you been cooking for?"

"Mr. Jason and Sam come several times a week for the noon meal and of course there is your mother's driver as well as the groundskeeper and the maids. I do miss cooking for Miss Ellie and Sally, but I'm sure they will return soon and things will get back to normal."

Normal? Nothing here would ever be normal again. His parents were the heart and soul of this house and now they were gone. Even if Ellie returns here, how long will she stay? There were several young men in Loveland who were interested in seeing her. One day, in the near future, she'll get married, and this will no longer be her home. That left him and who knows where he'd be practicing medicine once he graduated. There was no need for a doctor here or in Carson City. Even if he practiced in Reno, he'd want to live closer to his work than here.

"I hope so, Connie, but times are changing, and I'm afraid we are as well."

"I understand. Without Mr. and Mrs. Martin, the house doesn't feel the same. One day this will belong to someone else, but for now I like to pretend it will once again be the happy house I came to twenty-five years ago when I was a young girl. Before Mr. Jason had this house built for Mr. and Mrs. Martin, I cooked at The Mother Lode. It was Mr. Jason who asked me to come here and cook for your family. I've always been afraid I'd die first and leave your family without a cook. Whatever happens, I've done my job and I'm more than ready to retire and let someone else do the work."

On an impulse he hugged Connie tightly. He'd eaten her cooking every day of his life until he went away to school. It was then he appreciated the good food he equated with home.

* * * *

It seemed like every day another lawyer came to the mansion in St. Louis, requiring Amy's signature on one paper or another. She always thought if she and her mother had the money she'd been told her grandfather accumulated, they'd be happy. Now she was beginning to understand the reason for her grandfather's mood.

He'd told her there would be people to deal with the day-to-day running of his companies, and she could live comfortably. If this was comfortable, she wished she was scratching for a living the way her mother and she had for the fifteen years they lived in Loveland.

The thought crossing her mind reminded her of the time she's spent with Clay Martin. For the first weeks she'd been in St. Louis, he sent wires almost daily, but she'd been so busy with her grandfather many of them went unanswered.

The sound of someone at the door vaguely registered in her mind. She'd made the mistake of hurrying to answer the door when she first came here to live, only to be admonished by her grandfather's butler. He'd told her answering the door was his responsibility, and she should wait until visitors were announced before running to the door like a silly child.

"Miss Baines," the butler said when he entered the study where she was trying to decipher the numerous pages of figures one of the previous lawyers brought her two days earlier. "Mr. Harrison is here to see you."

Of all the lawyers who came to the mansion George was the one she trusted above all the others. "Please show him in, William."

Remembering the lessons her grandfather taught her, she remained seated when George entered the study.

"It's good to see you, Amy," George said, extending his hand in greeting.

"Oh, George you have no idea how good it is to see you. I can't believe the number of lawyers who have come to this house with papers for me to sign. Before he died, my grandfather told me I wouldn't be responsible for the day-to-day operation of his companies. At this point I'm so overwhelmed with all this paperwork I wish I'd never heard of Montgomery Palter and his money."

"Please calm yourself, Amy. I wish you had told me what was going on earlier. I could have taken all this off your shoulders. I just learned of all this. You can thank William for contacting me. I've been in touch with everyone concerned. I came here today to ask you to come down to the headquarters of Palter Shipping for a meeting of the board of directors tomorrow."

"Why is my presence requested now, when I've been inundated with paperwork here at the house for the last two months?"

"I must admit, all of this has been my fault. I was instructed to have everything changed over to your name with no paperwork being sent to you, but my office staff didn't follow through. The meeting tomorrow is to rectify the problem."

Amy still didn't understand George's explanation. "Why has this been left to your staff? I'm sure my grandfather was one of your biggest clients, as I am now."

"Please calm yourself, Amy. You're right, your grandfather, as well as you, are major clients of my office, but not our only clients. My partner and I have split the duties of your account for many years. I've been in court for the last month and just now learned what was going on here."

George crossed the room and took her hand in his. "The last thing either your grandfather or I wanted was for you to have to deal with anything other than living comfortably on your inheritance."

"Am I to assume tomorrow's meeting will change all of this?"

"My dear Amy, haven't you ever been told to never assume anything, but in this case you're right. I know you haven't been happy in St. Louis. I have been talking to some of our other clients, and I have a very good offer on this house."

"You mean someone wants to buy this property?"

"Most certainly, and they are prepared to pay you handsomely for it."

"What about the furnishings and William, to say nothing of the cook and the maids? How can I think of selling this place and taking away their livelihood? I would feel like a heartless witch."

She could hardly believe her ears when George began to laugh at her statement. "You are such a naïve young lady. I would never make a deal with anyone without considering the staff that runs this house efficiently. Even if the prospective buyers hadn't agreed to keep them on, trusted employees like these wouldn't ever have a problem finding a new position. Over the years each of them has been offered other positions, but remained loyal to this household."

* * * *

It was amazing how quickly everything went. By the first of

December, Amy was no longer plagued with the mounds of paperwork required to run Montgomery's various companies. In addition, the mansion had been sold, the servants were assured of their positions with the new owners, and the furnishings were auctioned off.

The fact she was a wealthy young woman was one thing, but in reality, she had nowhere to go and no one who cared if she came or went. Out of desperation, she purchased a ticket to Loveland. It was the only home she'd ever known. With luck she could find a place to buy as well as get her old job back.

The first person she saw when she arrived was Phil, the stationmaster for the railroad. "Amy! You're the last person I expected to see arriving today. What are you doing back here? I thought you were living in St. Louis."

Amy smiled at her old friend. "It's a long story. I'm sure you heard about me finding my grandfather and his passing. I've spent the past few months dealing with the fortune he left me. I finally got everything straightened out and sold the house as well as the furnishings. It was then I realized I had nowhere to go, so I decided to come home. I was wondering if you needed a telegraph operator."

"I wish I could say I did, but I filled the available positions months ago. Until I took over after your mother was attacked, I didn't realize how much work the two of you did. It took four men to replace you. The question I have is why would you want to work? With your resources you can do anything you want."

"That's just it. The only thing I know is working in the telegraph office. I can't imagine living an idle life. Maybe I can find a place to live here in Loveland and decide what I'm going to do."

"Why don't you hire a vehicle and drive out to the Tyler farm? You seemed to be comfortable staying out there this summer."

"Oh, I couldn't. If I'm right, they're dealing with a new baby and ..."

"And nothing," Eli said from behind her. "I came into town to see if new stallion I bought at an auction last week arrived on today's train. Even if he did arrive, I think the shipment standing in front of me is the most welcome one I could receive."

"Now just what are you talking about, Eli Tyler?" Amy said before allowing him to take her in his arms and give her a brotherly hug.

"Ma and Pa decided Becky and I needed some time alone with the baby so they went to Peoria to spend Christmas with Laura and her family. Unfortunately, Becky is getting tired. I know she would appreciate you coming out to the farm with me to help her out."

"What happened to Clay's sister and her friend? The last I knew they were staying with you while Clara went to be with Laura when her baby was born."

"We can talk about it on our way out to the farm. How much luggage to you have?"

"Just a trunk that has to be unloaded and my traveling bag. I'm afraid I indulged myself a little too much when I was in St. Louis. It was strange to be able to have a seamstress come and make me a new wardrobe and not have to worry about the cost."

"Good then you'll have lots of things to share with Becky when we get home. Give me a minute to check on my new stallion and then we'll head out to the farm."

Amy was pleased to see Eli brought a closed carriage into town today. With the weather becoming colder it was more than practical especially considering he would be bringing a new horse home with him.

She thought about the fact someone actually wanted her. At one time, she thought the man who wanted her was Clay. With all the work she had to do in St. Louis, first caring for her grandfather and then coming to grips with her new wealth, she'd closed the door on anything that might have been. If only she hadn't gone in search of the man she feared most of her life and learned to love at the end of his days, maybe she and Clay might have developed a relationship. Of course, it could have come to nothing considering she was far from his equal.

From the corner of her eye, Amy saw Eli coming toward the carriage leading a magnificent Clydesdale stallion.

"He's beautiful. Were you able to get my trunk?"

"Since I have the closed carriage, I arranged to have it delivered. I know this is one Christmas present Becky is going to be thrilled to get."

A light snow started falling before they made it to the farm making Amy glad for the closed carriage with a warm robe to put over her legs.

Although she'd only been gone a matter of weeks, the farm looked almost alien after being in the sophisticated world of St. Louis society.

Unlike the fabulous mansion her grandfather offered her, this was where she belonged. She didn't have the schooling or the social graces to fit into her grandfather's world. She'd led too sheltered a life in Loveland to even know how to act around people she considered her betters.

While Eli went out to take care of the horses, Amy picked up her traveling bag and made her way up the steps leading to the front porch. Without knocking, she entered Becky's warm kitchen and called out to her friend.

"Are you home, Becky?" she called, knowing the answer to her question.

"Amy? Is that you, Amy? Where did you come from? When did you get here?"

Amy rushed to where her friend stood and embraced her without wanting to let go. She was home and nothing else mattered.

"I left St. Louis and came directly here. I needed to come home. It was lucky for me that Eli was looking for a new horse to come in on the same train as I did. Otherwise I don't know what I would have done. I asked Phil for my old job back, but he'd already filled the position."

"I can't believe with all your money you even want to go back to work."

"What else would I do? I've worked with my ma ever since I was old enough to take the messages. I don't know anything else in my life."

"Well, I'm glad there wasn't a job for you in town. I'm thrilled to have you staying with us for a while. With the new baby, I seem to be tired all the time."

"Speaking of the baby, I don't even know if you had a boy or a girl."

"We had a little boy. We named him Robert after my grandfather. Luckily, he's sleeping right now so we can have some time together. Would you like a cup of coffee?"

Amy agreed and sat down at the familiar kitchen table. It seemed so normal to be sitting in her friend's kitchen and talking about things with little meaning to anyone but themselves. How different from the days she took coffee alone in either the library or the study of the mansion. This is what she missed the most during her time in St. Louis. This and getting to know Clay. At least she was getting back some semblance of normalcy even if Clay was out of her reach.

Chapter Nineteen

"I wish you were coming home for Christmas," Ellie whined when Clay told her he had to stay in San Francisco and be on call at the hospital.

"It not like I'm in private practice and have some control over the hours I work. I'm still in school and have to do what I'm told. Besides, the trains aren't even running to Virginia City because of the amount of snow in the mountain passes. In another six months, I'll finish with school and we can get together before I decide where to practice. By that time, I'll be more than ready to come home and relax. I've already had some good offers and it will give me time to come to a definite conclusion."

Clay continued to listen to how sick of the snow his sister was and how isolated she felt. He understood all of her complaints. Winter never bothered her before, but this would be her first Christmas without their parents. Like Ellie, he was fighting the feeling of loss that was growing within his mind.

There had been many times when he couldn't get home from school for the holidays because of the depth of the snow in the mountains. During those times he'd always looked forward to going to the student lounge to take a phone call from his parents to ease the pain of loneliness. This year, he enjoyed the luxury of speaking to his sister in private. He was pleased to find a telephone installed in his dorm room. The Dean told him it was necessary, at his level of study, to have a phone for emergencies that might arise at the hospital. Clay understood the necessity and agreed to be responsible for the bill should any long distance calls be made on it.

In the past, he'd been invited to the homes of his friends from school who lived in California and were more than happy to open their homes to a student who couldn't be with their families for Christmas. This year would be different. Since he was working in the hospital, he wouldn't be able to leave the dorm because he was working a double shift and would be too exhausted even to celebrate the holiday.

Before turning in to catch a few hours of sleep prior to heading to the hospital, he thought of Amy. The last time he'd heard from her was just before he left Loveland to return home and then move on to San Francisco. At that time, she was trying to deal with her grandfather's estate. He wondered if she was still struggling with it, or if she'd found a young man who wanted her to be his wife.

Just last week, he'd sent her a wire. Not having her telephone number, he knew the more archaic route would be the best. To his dismay, the wire was returned as undeliverable. In the matter of less than four months, she had simply disappeared, and he had no way to find her.

School was so demanding, he hadn't even had the time to contact Eli and see if he'd heard anything from her. As he fell asleep, he vowed when the holidays were over he'd send a letter to his cousin and make his inquiry.

* * * *

As the clock struck midnight, Amy sat alone in the Tyler living room watching the twinkling electric lights on the Christmas tree standing in the corner. This would be her first real Christmas. When her mother was alive this was just another day. There were no church services nor were there any of the other trappings of the holiday in their home. Of course, she always received a gift from her mother and gave one in return, but that was the extent of their celebration.

The few weeks she'd spent with her grandfather opened her eyes to many things, including the beauty of the gift God gave to His children when he sent his only begotten Son on Christmas. Tonight's service at the church drove the message home as she heard the Christmas story read from the Bible.

God did give the world a wonderful gift. She knew she was not too late to receive it and come back into His loving embrace. Learning her parents had her baptized was the key that unlocked her heart. She yearned for the strength to learn more about God's love and to find the path He wanted her to follow.

Her silent prayer finished, she rose and unplugged the lights adorning the Christmas tree. Trying to be as quiet as possible, she made her way to bed, so as not to waken the rest of the sleeping family. She'd just gotten into her room when she heard someone outside her door.

"I waited until I heard you come to bed," Becky whispered as she followed Amy into the room.

"What are you doing up? I thought you went to bed long ago."

"We did, but we had to wait for you to go to bed before Eli could go downstairs and play Santa Claus. I realize Robert is too little to understand, but it's a tradition, both in Eli's family and mine."

Amy thought back to when she'd been a little girl going to school and heard her friends talk about how much they were looking forward to a visit from Santa Claus. She'd asked her mother about the tradition and was told it was nothing they celebrated in their home.

This was her first real Christmas. She begged God to give her the gift of knowledge as to what she should be doing with her life.

* * * *

Amy woke to delicious smells coming from the kitchen. Over the past few weeks, she'd helped Becky make dozens of cookies as well as candies the likes she'd never knew existed.

She luxuriated in the warmth of her bed as she reviewed the dream she's experienced. In it she stood on the deck of one of her grandfather's ships sailing to she didn't know where.

Was God trying to tell her she should learn Grandfather's business, or should she consider using some of her money to travel? Her silent plea to God went unanswered. Being so new to knowing God and trying to understand his ways, she laughed at her questions. God wasn't going to answer her. She would be the one to interpret the dream and decide what it meant for her future.

After washing up and dressing for the day, she hurried downstairs to see if she could help Becky with any of the preparations for Christmas dinner. Even with Gary and Clara in Peoria, there would be company as Becky's parents were expected for the noon meal.

Entering the living room, Amy was surprised to see brightly wrapped presents where just last night a tree skirt was the only thing on the floor under the tree.

"What's all this?" she said.

"I told you last night, Santa Claus came. As soon as Eli finishes with the chores we'll have breakfast and then open presents. Of course, Robert doesn't know what's going on, but in the future he'll look forward to this tradition. I know Eli's parents always exchange gifts on Christmas Eve, but we decided to start a new practice for our family."

Amy thought about the gifts she'd purchased for Becky, Eli, and Robert the last time she went to town. She'd even bought the Christmas paper as well as the colored string the storekeeper suggested she buy. After looking at the gifts Becky placed under the tree, she knew her first efforts at trying to wrap presents looked more like something done by a young child than by a grown woman.

"I have to go back up to my room and get my gifts for you."

"Oh, Amy, you shouldn't have spent your money on us. Just having you staying with us is a perfect gift."

"Nonsense. This morning I was thinking how this is my first Christmas. Ma was so bitter about how she was treated by my grandfather, she shunned anything that had to do with Christianity. She always gave me a gift, because as she said, she didn't want me to be any different from the children in my class at school. Of course, we both knew I was different. I wish I'd known the Lord earlier in my life. It would have made forgiveness of my grandfather much easier."

By the time Amy returned to the kitchen, Eli sat at the table, holding Robert in his arms while Becky made what she called yellow bread for their breakfast. Amy watched as her friend dipped thick slices of homemade bread into the milk and egg mixture before putting it on the griddle. A hit of cinnamon combined with the aroma of the frying bread to make her mouth water.

"Merry Christmas," Eli greeted her. "You're in for a real treat. Becky makes the best yellow bread I've ever tasted. Ma used to make it on special occasions, but I think the cinnamon she uses is what makes the difference. At least that's what Ma says."

Becky brought plates of the delightful looking treat to the table. Amy watched as Becky slathered her bread with butter and then sprinkled on confectioner's sugar, while Eli used honey in place of the sugar.

"Which way is the best way to eat this?" Amy sought guidance.

"It's really personal preference," Becky replied. "My dad likes to tradeoff between sorghum and maple syrup. I prefer the sugar, and, as you can see, Eli uses honey. If you'd like sorghum or syrup I can get it for you."

"I think I'll try eating mine like you do. It looks much lighter than the honey."

They enjoyed the rest of the meal but before Amy and Becky could clean up the kitchen Eli suggested they go into the living room and open presents.

Amy questioned his decision, since they only had a few hours before Becky's parents were due to arrive for Christmas dinner, and she didn't like leaving the kitchen in a mess. If Becky had the same concerns, she didn't express them. Instead she seemed anxious to accompany Eli into the living room to attack the presents stacked under the tree.

Amy soon learned most of the gifts were for Robert with one gift each for Eli, Becky, and Amy in the pile under the tree. After adding hers, Amy delighted in seeing how excited Becky was over the Santa Claus gifts Robert received, even though she'd been the one who purchased and wrapped them.

Tears formed in Amy's eyes as she opened the gift she'd received from Becky and Eli. She gasped at the beauty of the ornate gold cross on a slender chain. "Oh this is too much."

"Nonsense," Eli replied. "When Ma and Pa learned of your acceptance of God, they said this was exactly what you needed. We all went in on it, and Pa had it made especially for you in Peoria. I got it in the mail just a couple of days ago. It goes along with this." He handed her another package, this one much larger.

As soon as she opened the box, she gasped at the beautiful leather bound Bible. The one her grandfather left her was worn from years of reading. The pages of this one were crisp and new as though they were waiting for her to explore them for herself. She opened the cover and read the inscription

To Amy—Let the journey begin—With Love—Eli and Becky
Christmas 1915.

"I'll treasure this always," she promised, as she got to her feet to embrace the friends who stood by her during this, the most trying time of her life.

"I think this is the time for me to tell you what I've decided to do after the first of the year. My grandfather told me I could do anything I wanted with my newfound wealth. What I've decided to do is to travel to New Orleans and see his shipping business for myself. I've learned they take passengers, and I think it would be a good way to learn what the shipping line is doing so I can better understand how the managers are handling the company."

"Alone?" Becky's voice carried shock and disbelief.

"With the exception of my mother, I've been alone all my life. I think an ocean voyage will give me the time I need to decide on what to do with the rest of my life."

Chapter Twenty

Clay read the letter from his cousin, Eli, for what seemed like the hundredth time. Amy hadn't stayed in St. Louis as he thought she might. Instead, she'd been in Loveland for Christmas and left just after the first of the year to sail on one of her grandfather's ships to a destination she didn't disclose. Knowing the extent of her grandfather's shipping empire, she could be anywhere in the world. From what Clay learned, the ships went to Europe, the Orient, and South America in addition to the east and west coasts of the United Stated.

With graduation only two days away, he was now rethinking his plans to interview for positions in the St. Louis area. There would be no need to look for something in a town when the woman, he'd come to realize he loved, was no longer there.

Setting aside the letter, he picked up the stack of requests he'd had from hospitals and clinics all over the country. These were the ones he'd set aside when his concentration had been completely on St. Louis.

He immediately rejected requests from big cities like New York, Philadelphia, and Chicago. He now realized he would much rather be in a more rural setting. The ones left came from Omaha, Reno, Spokane, and Albuquerque. He set pen to paper and wrote letters requesting interviews at each of the hospitals.

Unlike many of his classmates, he wasn't struggling financially. The inheritance he'd received from his parents left him in a comfortable position where finding a job could take as long as six months until he found the perfect match.

The ringing of the phone jolted him back to the reality of how quickly time could pass. Undoubtedly it was his sister calling to tell him she and Sally finally arrived at the hotel he'd arranged for them to stay in while they were in San Francisco for the graduation.

"Hello," he said.

"Is this Clay Martin?" a woman's voice on the other end of the line inquired.

He tried to recognize the voice, but to no avail. "Yes, this is Clay Martin. I'm afraid you have me at a disadvantage."

"This is Erma Wallace from the administrative office of the university. We have had a request from someone wanting to contact you. I needed to be sure I would be doing the right thing in giving out your information."

"Who is it that wanted to know about me?"

"She didn't give me a name, but she was an attractive young lady. When I said I didn't feel comfortable doing something like that, she told me she would get the information from somewhere else."

"You did what you felt was best, Mrs. Wallace. If I had been in your position I would have done the same thing. Thank you for looking out for my best interests."

He took a moment to think about Erma Wallace. He'd met her when he first enrolled at the university. She struck him as the grandmother he never knew. She was probably in her mid to late fifties with grey hair she wore in a fashionable bob. As far as the rest of her appearance was concerned, she always wore the latest fashion even though he knew she was a widow dependent on her job for her livelihood.

Still thinking about the mystery woman who asked Erma for his information, he got ready for work and prepared for his shift in the emergency room. Hopefully, by the time he finished, Ellie and Sally would have arrived at the hotel and he could relax. This was his last shift at the hospital prior to graduation. The grueling hours of seeing patients would be over, and he could wait for the letters he hoped would arrive. Since he would be returning to Virginia City with Ellie and Sally, he planned to have responses sent to his home rather than the dorm.

* * * *

Halfway through his shift at the hospital, Clay was surprised to be called to the front desk. Once there, he broke into a wide grin seeing Ellie and Sally waiting for him.

"Hi, big brother," Ellie greeted him as she rushed to throw her arms around his neck. "When we didn't get an answer at your dorm room, we took a chance you were working and came to you."

"I'm glad you did. Have you been to the hotel?"

"Of course we have, child," Sally responded.

"We were able to book two more rooms," Ellie continued. "It's supposed to be a surprise, but you know I can't keep a secret. Jason and Sam came with us. Jason said there was no way he was going to miss your graduation, and he has a special gift for you. I don't know what it is, but you know Jason, whatever it is, it's big."

The thought of Jason making the trip from Virginia City to San Francisco for his special day was exciting and at the same time frightening. "I didn't think Jason was in the best of health. Are you sure he should have made this trip?"

"I said the same thing to Mr. Jason," Sally said. "He told me he's feeling much better, and if I thought he was going to stay in Virginia City while you're graduating out here, I was out of my mind. He was excited on the train trip, but Sam insisted he stay at the hotel and rest."

"I agree, and it's my opinion as a doctor, the two of you should go back to the hotel and get some rest too. This is my last shift, and I won't be finished until late tonight. I'll meet you at the hotel tomorrow morning at eight for breakfast."

"Are you sure about meeting us so early?" Ellie looked doubtful. "If you're not getting off until late this evening, don't you need more sleep?"

"I'll have lots of time to sleep after graduation on Saturday. I'm used to working two shifts in a row and getting by with very little sleep. I promise I'll see you in the morning."

* * * *

Amy left the administrative office of the university. She was disappointed when the woman at the desk refused to give her any information on how she could find Clay. The only good thing to come out of her visit was learning he would be graduating on Saturday, and

Outlaw's Secrets

she intended to be there.

She thought of how much she'd grown since leaving Loveland in January. Being a mild winter, she'd had no problem getting a train to New Orleans. Once there, she went to the office for the shipping line and introduced herself. It didn't take long for her to secure passage on a ship going through the newly opened Panama Canal to California.

She had to admit, she wasn't enamored with sea travel, but it was an experience. If this was how she was going to make a living for the rest of her life, she felt she needed to know about it firsthand.

While on board, she heard horror stories about rounding the Horn when getting from New Orleans to California. All were excited about the new Panama Canal and how easy the voyage was now, to say nothing of the amount of time it saved.

"You'll see, lassie," Captain MacDonald assured her. "This will be a calm voyage and the shorter time this takes will give your company a great profit. I must tell you it's a privilege to have you sailing with us on your first time aboard a ship."

With the ship only going as far as Los Angeles, Captain MacDonald was gracious enough to escort her to the train station so she could book passage to San Francisco.

It touched her heart when the crusty old sea captain waited until she boarded the train. Even from the window of her compartment, she could see him standing on the platform watching until the train pulled out of the station. Once she could no longer see him, she settled back and wiped a tear from her eye. Another chapter in her life was now closed. She doubted her path and that of Captain MacDonald would cross again. He'd been as kind to her as had everyone she'd met through her grandfather's companies.

The trip from Los Angeles seemed to go on forever with the train stopping at every small town along the way. Amy was glad she'd gotten a compartment. The time alone would be best spent if she concentrated on what she would do if Clay rejected her or perhaps had married during the months they'd been separated. It was entirely possible there was a special woman in San Francisco, and his attentions toward her had been out of compassion rather than attraction.

As she made her way back to the hotel where she'd booked a room, she again thought about the possibility of Clay already having a wife. If her assumptions proved to be right, she would pay her respects to the new doctor and decide what to do from here on.

So far she'd followed her heart and on her journey learned more about God and his plan for her.

Dear God, she prayed. Lead me in the right path. If Clay isn't meant to be in my future, help me to find a place for myself.

Chapter Twenty-One

Clay sat with his fellow classmates listening to the speeches being made by the members of the faculty as well as the invited guests. Even when he'd been working the long hours at the hospital, he'd never been as nervous as he was today. Once these ceremonies ended, he would be a doctor. Where he would be practicing medicine was still a mystery.

Dear God, please help me to understand what your plan for me is.

The silent prayer that formed in his mind came as a shock. As a child he prayed often, but always for selfish things like a new pony or perhaps a bicycle. Last summer he'd come to grips with his lost faith. At the time, he'd promised himself he'd get back into the practice of going to church and reestablishing his relationship with God. Unfortunately, once he returned to San Francisco it was much easier to fall back into his old routine. He had, once again, put God on the back burner.

The dean of the university began to call the names of the graduates. Clay paid close attention to the names of his friends and stood to walk across the stage to accept proof of not only his degree but also his ability to practice medicine.

"Ladies and Gentlemen," the dean said, once the last graduate shook hands and received his degree. "I give you the graduating class of 1916. Your professors and I wish you well wherever you go and whatever you do with your education."

Clay, along with his fellow graduates, cheered and congratulated each other on finally finishing their educations. Once he stepped into the May sunlight, he was met by Ellie, Jason, Sally, and Sam.

"We are so proud of you," Jason declared. "I have reservations at one of the best restaurants in San Francisco so we can go there to celebrate."

Clay accepted Jason's hand, shook hands with Sam, and hugged both Ellie and Sally tightly. From the corner of his eye, he saw a woman who resembled Amy burst into tears and turn from the crowd of people offering their congratulations.

Immediately he disentangled himself from his sister's embrace and pushed through the crown to get to the spot where he'd seen her standing moments earlier. To his dismay, she was nowhere to be seen. Pressing on, he finally caught a glimpse of her as she got into a cab and it pulled away, taking her further away from him than she'd been in the past few months.

* * * *

How could he? Amy knew it was possible he could be married. She just hadn't expected to see him hugging and kissing his wife in public. By the time she reached the street, she was able to hail a cab.

"Where to, Miss?" the driver asked.

She tried to compose herself enough to give the man the name of her hotel. As the cab pulled away from the curb, she saw Clay break from the crowd. Had he come to find her, or to tell her there was no need in her staying in San Francisco?

Rather than take a chance on being rejected, she said nothing more to the driver and settled back to enjoy the ride to her hotel. From there she could send a wire to Captain MacDonald and find out when the next ship would sail from Los Angeles to New Orleans.

After paying the cab driver, she hurried to her room. She didn't even stop at the desk until someone called her name. She turned to see Captain MacDonald waiting for her in the lobby.

"I was worried about you lass. It didn't take me long to secure a load to bring to San Francisco. Since I knew where you said you'd be saying I booked myself a room. I just couldn't stand the thought of you being alone in a city the size of this one. We don't sail for another week."

"Oh, Captain, I am so happy to see you. I went to the graduation today, and he was there with his wife. I ran away. This was such a bad idea. I know now I should go back to St. Louis, buy myself a little house and go back to Grandfather's office and see if I can secure a position with the company."

"Don't be too hasty, lassie. It's possible things aren't always as they seem. We have a week to see the sights and put everything into perspective. It's close to suppertime. Will you allow me the pleasure of taking you out to eat?"

Amy relaxed. Instead of being alone in a strange town she would have a trusted friend to be with her until it was time to sail back to New Orleans.

"I'd like that. Give me a minute to go up to my room and change my clothes and I'll meet you down here let's say an hour."

* * * *

"What was that all about?" Ellie demanded when Clay returned back to where his family stood.

"I saw Amy. She was here, but when she saw me hugging you, she turned and left. I got to where she'd been standing, I saw her get into a cab. She could be anywhere. I've lost her."

"Did you get the name of the cab company?" Jason asked.

"I ... I don't think so. I know it was a big black Chrysler, and it had a number ten painted on the door."

"It shouldn't be hard to track her down. Tomorrow morning you and Sam can go down to the cab companies and see what you can find."

"Tomorrow morning," Clay echoed. "By then she could be anywhere. I have to find her now. I can't let her get away from me again."

Jason put his hand on Clay's shoulder. "If it was her, she must be staying in San Francisco. As I said earlier, we'll contact the cab company in the morning, and they should be able to help us to find her. For now, let's go back to the dorm and pick up your belongings. It's time you moved to the hotel and joined us as a tour guide for this marvelous city."

Defeated, Clay agreed and went with the others to where they could catch a cab. His own automobile was still at the dorm and would accommodate him and Ellie while the others took a cab back to the hotel. His belongings had been packed and all he had to do was speak to the janitor about having them transferred to the hotel as well.

"Oh dear," Ellie lamented when they entered the room Clay called home for the past five years. "How could you stand to live in such a confined space? This is just dreadful."

Clay looked at his surroundings. He never considered it to be confining. Even with a roommate, they both had enough space to store their belongings, have study time and be able to sleep at night.

"Guess I never looked at it that way before. With all my classes and work at the hospital, I was just glad to have a place to lay my head at night."

"Well, I'm glad I never went to college. There is no way I could survive in a space this small, to say nothing of having to share a bathroom with God only knows how many other girls. It's enough to make me sick to my stomach."

Clay laughed at her. It was evident she should be on the lookout for a very rich husband who could make all her dreams come true. Even with his status as a doctor, he doubted he would ever enjoy all the luxuries his parents provided for him as he grew up.

Chapter Twenty-Two

Amy fussed with her hair and smoothed her dress out before leaving her room to join Captain MacDonald for supper. People would think she was a silly schoolgirl getting ready to go out with a young man for the first time. The captain was old enough to be her father. Once the thought crossed her mind, she shook her head to rid herself of it. The captain was only being kind and looking out for her best interests. She was, in fact, his employer.

As soon as she stepped into the lobby of the hotel, she saw him waiting for her. He looked far different from the man she saw only an hour earlier. He'd shaved his unruly beard and trimmed his hair. Dressed in a tight fitting dress uniform, he looked much younger than she originally thought him. Dashing was the word that immediately entered her mind.

"Good evening, lassie," he greeted her. "Are you ready to go to supper with me?"

"Yes, Captain. I would be honored to have you escort me."

"And I would be honored if you'd call me by my given name, Sean, when I'm not on duty."

Amy smiled. "Then Sean it is, but only if you call me Amy."

He took her hand and tucked it into the cook of his arm as he escorted her toward the dining room just off the lobby of the hotel.

"When I checked in, the man at the desk said this is one of the best restaurants in the city," Sean said, as he escorted her to a table set for two.

It was obvious many of the guests of the hotel ate here, and she was glad she'd taken time to put on one of the fancy dresses she'd purchased in New Orleans especially for this trip. She'd hoped to be wearing this particular dress when she and Clay dined together tonight, but with his wife waiting for him, she knew her dream evening wasn't going to happen. She thanked God for the fact Sean followed her so she wouldn't be eating alone in her room tonight.

The food, as promised, was excellent. She was midway through her main course and thoroughly enjoying not only her entree but also Sean's company when she saw them enter the room.

"Are you alright, Amy?" Sean inquired. "You look as though you've seen a ghost. Is there something wrong with your food?"

"I'm sorry, Sean, I'm feeling suddenly faint. If you'll excuse me, I must go to my room and rest."

"Allow me to escort you."

"No, I couldn't ask you to miss your meal. Please finish without me. Since you're staying at this hotel, I'll contact you in the morning. I'd love to see the sights and don't relish doing so on my own. Thank you for a lovely evening."

* * * *

Ellie and Sally bubbled with joy as they talked of the dinner they planned for tonight in the hotel's dining room. Clay knew he should be pleased with the party they were orchestrating in his honor, but being within mere feet of Amy, only to lose her, dampened his spirits. Feigning excitement, he followed them into the dining room and held Ellie's chair as she seated herself to the right of the head of the table, indicating his was the place of honor.

As soon as he took his seat, he saw Amy sitting across the room with an older man. To his horror, the color drained from her face and she got up from the table and hurried out of the room. He started to get to his feet, but stopped when Jason gave him the look that said he would handle things.

Clay watched as Jason crossed the room to speak with the older man sitting at the table Amy just left. He wished he knew the identity of the man with whom Amy was having supper.

"Where's Jason going?" Ellie said.

"I saw Amy sitting with a gentleman on the other side of the room. Before I could go to her, she left the room. I need to find her ..."

"Sit down, Clay," Jason interrupted when he returned to the table. "The man at the table is Captain Sean MacDonald. He works for Amy's grandfather's shipping line. She came to California in search of you on his ship. It was his concern that prompted him to follow her to San Francisco. Amy told him she saw you and Ellie together and assumed the two of you were married."

"Then I have to see her now, more than I did before. She has to know the truth."

"She will, but she's not ready to see you tonight. Captain MacDonald suggested we meet him for breakfast in the morning and straighten everything out."

* * * *

Amy awoke, her head pounding and her eyes burning from the amount of tears she shed before finally going to sleep. The fancy party dress lay crumpled on the floor. Rather than wearing her crisp nightgown to bed, she'd slept in her underclothes from the night before.

The sun was just beginning to rise, showing the wispy fog rolling in from the bay. She glanced at the mantle clock resting above the marble fireplace that graced her room. She knew she'd paid far too much for her accommodations, but Sean insisted she should reserve a reputable hotel since she would be all alone in the city.

Reluctantly she got out of bed and made her way to the bathroom adjacent to her room. After bathing, she scrubbed her face and brushed her teeth. The reflection in the mirror looked as it had every morning of her life, except her eyes were still red from the tears she'd shed. It didn't take her long to run a comb through her hair and finish dressing for the day.

As planned, she made her way down to the lobby to inquire about Sean's room number. For his sake, she would put on a happy face and explore this fascinating city. With luck he could obtain another load to take to New Orleans, and they could be on their way back home before the end of the week.

"Good morning, Miss Baines," the desk clerk greeted her.

"Good morning," she replied. "I was wondering if I could have you get a message to Captain Sean MacDonald."

"Ah, yes, Captain MacDonald. He left a message for you this morning."

The young man handed her an envelope. Taking it, she felt her heart sink as her hands began to shake. "Thank you," she managed to say before going to one of the elegant couches in the sitting area of the lobby.

He'd left San Francisco without her. She couldn't blame him. She sure made a fool out of herself last night when she saw Clay come in with his wife. With trepidation, she opened the envelope. Inside the note was written in a bold and fancy script, one she would never equate with a sea captain.

> *Amy—Please join me in the dining room for breakfast. We can plan our day and come to a decision about your future.— Sean*

He hadn't left her. Her inner voice practically sang the words over and over again. She carefully folded the note and put it in the pocket of her skirt. Getting to her feet, she hurried toward the dining room. All her life she'd wanted a father and Sean was as close to that as she was ever going to get.

Sean waited for her just inside the door to the dining room. "Have you been waiting for me long?"

"Not long. I'm glad you accepted my invitation." Acting like the gentleman he'd been the night before, he took her hand, tucked it in the crook of his arm and escorted her as though she was a queen through the crowded dining room.

To her surprise, rather than stopping at one of the tables set for two, he took her to a large table in a secluded nook of the room. As soon as she approached the table, Clay got to his feet.

"Don't even think about running away from me this time," he said. "I'd like you to meet my family."

"I saw your wife yesterday at the graduation. I can accept the fact you're married, but I'm not interested in making polite conversation with the woman you love." Sean's grip tightened on her hand, keeping her from fleeing as she had the night before.

"Please, Amy, hear us out," the woman she saw with Clay yesterday said as she touched Amy's free hand. "Clay is very important in my life, but not because he's my husband. Clay is my brother. I'm Ellie, and I've heard so much about you, both from my brother and my cousins. By the time I got to Loveland, you were already in St. Louis."

"S ... sister." Amy stammered. "I thought ..."

"I know what you thought," Clay said. It was evident he was trying hard not to be too emotional. "I was looking at positions in the St. Louis area, but Eli told me you'd left for New Orleans to sail with one of your grandfather's ships. I knew then I'd lost you, because you could have gone anywhere in the world."

"But I didn't go anywhere exotic. I came to California and took a train from Los Angeles to San Francisco to find you."

"So Sean told us last night. Thank goodness he followed you here to look out for your best interests. If he hadn't, we might not have found you. I told you last summer I wanted to get to know you better. I haven't changed my mind. Maybe it's a good thing I haven't taken a position yet. I'm still waiting for letters back from some of the hospitals I've contacted. During that time, we can get better acquainted, that is if you would be willing to come back to Virginia City with us."

Amy felt all the tension drain from her body. "Are you sure you want me to come to Virginia City? It's been almost a year and ..."

"And I haven't stopped thinking of you for even one minute. I knew the moment I first saw you I wanted you to become someone special in my life. We've got a week before taking the train back home. I promised my family I'd show them the sights of San Francisco. I would be honored if you'd join us."

"Wh ... what about Sean?"

"His ship doesn't sail until the end of the week. He's agreed to join us. He says someone needs to chaperone you."

Amy smiled and allowed Clay to hold her chair at the place next to his at the head of the table.

* * * *

Clay felt as though he was a child opening his Christmas presents. The one person he wanted in his life and was afraid he'd lost now sat to his right. At any moment he could reach out and touch her, and the dream he'd kept alive for the last year finally came true.

"I propose a toast," Jason said getting to his feet, once they all had large glasses of fresh squeezed orange juice in their hands. "To Dr. Clay Martin. May he serve his patients well."

Around the table everyone echoed their well wishes with the phrase, "Here, Here!"

"Yesterday I told Clay I had a special surprise for him. Once he returns to Virginia City, there is a new clinic with the latest equipment waiting for him."

"A modern clinic in Virginia City?"

Jason smiled at Clay's question. "This has been in the planning ever since you left for your first day at school. Dr. Carlton told us several years ago he would only stay on until someone could be trained to take his place. Since your mother knew of your desire, she decided to finance your education in return for Dr. Carlton's agreement to stay. If you will take the position, he will be leaving as of the first of June."

Clay thought about the opportunity he was being offered. He would be able to stay in the area where he grew up and serve the people he'd loved all his life.

"Of course I'll take it, on one condition."

Around the table everyone's eyes mirrored surprise at Clay's statement.

"What would that condition be?" Jason said.

Clay took Amy's hand in his. "I'll be happy to accept your offer if at the end of the summer, Amy would consider relocating to Virginia City."

Amy's smile was the only confirmation he needed.

"Something tells me, you have your answer, Big Brother," Ellie said. "It looks like I'm going to have a new sister-in-law soon."

* * * *

Amy never imagined she'd be seeing the sights with not only Clay but also his family. She was saddened when they took Sean down to the docks when it was time for him to leave for New Orleans.

"When I get back to home port, I will be retiring from the sea."

"Retiring?" Amy echoed. "But you're so good at what you do. Why would you want to retire, especially now with the Panama Canal open?"

"I have other aspirations with the company. I only stayed on board because the company insisted they had to find someone who could take my place. I had a wire waiting for me in Los Angeles saying my replacement was ready for when I returned to New Orleans."

"What will you do?" Clay asked.

"I've been offered a position in the head office, securing loads and looking into more profitable routes. After this trip, when I was able to pick up cargo in Los Angeles to San Francisco, I was certain this was what I wanted to do within the company."

"I'm sorry to hear you're leaving the sea," Amy lamented. "Of course, you aren't leaving the company. You will be able to continue to look out for my best interests."

Although she didn't want to say goodbye to Sean, she knew he was following his heart and wished him a bon voyage and waved as he boarded the ship.

Chapter Twenty-Three

Although Amy was sad to see Sean leave the city, she soon became fast friends with Ellie and Sally. All her life she'd wanted a sister, and in Ellie she found the female companionship she'd missed since moving to St. Louis to care for her grandfather until the time of his death.

Sally became like another mother to her, and she enjoyed the amount of pampering she received. Having never had much contact with black people, the only thing she knew about them was what she'd read in the history books in school. Every myth she'd ever heard had been shattered by Sally's delightful personality.

By the time the train to Virginia City was ready to leave, Clay sold the car he told her he'd kept at school for the entire time he attended the University and worked at the hospital. Even with her newfound wealth, she wasn't prepared for how quickly things happened when Clay and Jason worked together.

On their last night in San Francisco, Clay insisted the two of them go out by themselves. At first, the request took her completely off guard. When she finally realized what he was asking, she could feel a warm glow filling her.

"Does this mean you're courting me?"

"I haven't done a lot of courting in my life, but I think that's what they call it. I told you I wanted to get to know you better, but it's a little hard with my entire family with us every time we're together. I'm falling in love with you, Amy, but how can I make you fall in love with me, if we have no time alone."

Amy took Clay's hand in hers. "I don't think you'll have to work very hard at making me fall in love with you, Clay Martin. I've been in love with you ever since you first walked into the telegraph office in Loveland. I knew I didn't stand a chance, but I enjoyed the fantasy. I can only hope that once we return to your home I'll be able to fit in."

"You're going to fit in perfectly. I'm sure the mountains will suit you very well, and the mansion will be the perfect home for us."

"Oh Clay, are you asking me to marry you?"

"I guess I am. There's a beautiful chapel not far from our house. My mother went there often, and as a child, so did I. This winter, I've been considering getting better acquainted with the Lord, but my responsibilities got in the way. I plan to do better once we get home. I hope you'll be able to accept that about me."

Amy laughed. "Haven't you noticed the cross I've been wearing? It was a gift from your family in Missouri. It came along with a Bible. They said it was time I had a Bible of my own, since the one my grandfather left me was so large it has hard to carry around. To be truthful, that Bible with many of the possessions I had in St. Louis have been in storage, just waiting for me to find a place I'd be comfortable living. Of course, the Bible I received at Christmas is packed with my belongings at the hotel."

"I can't believe we both decided to find the Lord at the same time. Of course you haven't answered my question. Will you marry me?"

Tears filled Amy's eyes as her heart did a quickened beat. "I didn't think you'd ever ask. I will be proud to be your wife, and I'm sure living in Virginia City will agree with me very well."

Epilogue

Virginia City, 1919

Amy sat on the veranda of the mansion she'd called home for the past three years. It took a few months for her to become used to living at such a high altitude and to having servants to do her bidding. For Ellie, it all came naturally. Amy found even having lived in her grandfather's mansion in St. Louis, she wasn't prepared to become the mistress of this vast house.

Within her belly, the baby kicked reminding her the next generation was waiting to be born within the next month. Over the past three years, she'd been pregnant three times, but this was the first one she'd carried full term. With all the others, she'd lost them early. This time had been different. Once she passed the magical fourth month, Clay insisted she not do anything but relax and allow others to do everything for her.

"Have you been taking things easy like I asked you to?" Clay said as he mounted the steps.

"You know I have."

"Good, because I just got some wonderful news. I received a letter today from Eli, and the entire family is planning a trip to come here for the baby's christening."

"How can they do that, with all the work on the farm?"

"Eli assured me that, with the war ending, there have been several men coming home and looking for work. They've been training hired hands so they can come out. Even Cousin Laura is coming with her family from Peoria."

"Oh, dear. Will we have enough room to accommodate all of them?"

"Jason assures me his hotel will have enough room for everyone who won't be able to stay here."

Amy got to her feet just as the first pains of labor hit. "Maybe it's a good thing they've already made their plans to come here, because this little one is ready to be born. You don't happen to know a good doctor, do you?" She winked at her husband as he helped her into the house.

It didn't take long for Ellie and Sally to come to the master bedroom and shoo Clay away. "We'll call you when you need you, Mr. Clay," Sally said in her most stern motherly voice.

Even though Ellie no longer lived in the mansion, Amy knew she'd be there for this special birth. Two years earlier, Ellie married Austin Clearwater, the teacher at the local school. Although Clay insisted they could remain living at the mansion, Ellie and Austin wanted a place of their own. As a wedding present, Jason had a home built for them, just down the road from the mansion.

Labor seemed to go on forever. In reality, it was only four hours before William Clay Martin came into the world screaming at the top of his lungs. It took only a matter of minutes for his twin sister, Della Amanda Martin to make her appearance.

"Twins?" Amy's voice was hardly more than a whisper.

She saw the amazement in Clay's eyes change to pride as he handed the second crying baby to Sally. "I'd say we got a bonus. It's hard to believe it, but we have two beautiful babies. I know it's been hard on you, Amy, but they're definitely worth the wait."

* * * *

Even in the mountains, August prove to be hot. Clay waited at the train station for his family to arrive. Everyone was excited to have the only living members of the Tyler family gathered for the first time.

One by one they stepped off the train and were taken either to The Mother Lode or the mansion. Eli and Becky as well as Laura and her family opted to stay at the mansion. Unlike the younger members of the family, Gary and Clara were anxious to get better acquainted with Jason.

For the church service on Sunday, the small chapel was filled with not only the Tyler family, but also the regular members of the congregation. The elite of Virginia City mingled with the Missouri and

Illinois members of Clay's family, as well as the miners and children from the orphanage.

It was a joyous occasion when William and Della were dedicated to God.

After the service, everyone was invited to the mansion for a party. Once there, it was Gary who got to his feet to make a toast.

"To my nephew, Clay and his lovely wife, Amy. May you forever live in the light of the Lord and raise your children to also follow His teachings. Now that all the secrets of the Tyler Gang have come to the forefront, may there be no more outlaw secrets in our family."

About the Author

Mild Mannered wife, mother, and grandmother by day, Sherry Derr-Wille spends her nights writing and writing and writing. Having been inspired by an English assignment in her sophomore year of high school, she had never quite finished the assignment. New stories pop into her head every day with never enough time to write them all.

A Wisconsin native, she grew up a country girl, but enjoys her 'city' home. She and her husband of almost 50 years, Bob, live in a mid-sized town close to the Illinois border, where they are both enjoying their retirement. Deeming Bob 'A Saint' for putting up with her she has never regretted marrying her high school sweetheart just two days after graduation in 1964.

www.derr-wille.com

**Read more by this author at
www.melange-books.com**

Hattie's Preacher, The Outlaw Series, Book 1
Outlaw's Son, The Outlaw Series, Book 2
Outlaw's Daughter, The Outlaw Series, Book 3

www.ingramcontent.com/pod-product-compliance
Lightning Source LLC
Chambersburg PA
CBHW052144170626
46812CB00004B/1581